MW00743900

THE SILENT CRY

2455-DRON

THE SILENT CRY

Kira Chase

2455-DRON

Copyright © 2000 by Kira Chase.

ISBN #: Softcover 0-7388-3273-1

All rights reserved. No part of this book may be reproduced or transmitted in any form or by any means, electronic or mechanical, including photocopying, recording, or by any information storage and retrieval system, without permission in writing from the copyright owner.

This is a work of fiction. Names, characters, places and incidents either are the product of the author's imagination or are used fictitiously, and any resemblance to any actual persons, living or dead, events, or locales is entirely coincidental.

This book was printed in the United States of America.

To order additional copies of this book, contact:
Xlibris Corporation
1-888-7-XLIBRIS
www.Xlibris.com
Orders@Xlibris.com

CONTENTS

To My Daughters – Thank you both
for your love, support, and understanding.

2455-DRON

CHAPTER ONE

She walked into the tavern, slowly made her way over to the bar and promptly ordered a double shot of whiskey. She held the drink with shaky hands, then tossed her head back, consuming the drink in one gulp. She wiped her mouth with the back of her hand and leaned her elbows on the bar as she looked around the dimly lit room. She recognized a few patrons but made no effort at a greeting. If anyone cared to speak to her, he or she would have to make the first move, though she doubted anyone would offer her a friendly word; they knew that when she was in a mood it was best to leave her alone.

She ordered another double as her gaze traveled to the opposite end of the bar and saw a familiar woman sitting there. She hadn't noticed her sitting there when she arrived. *Maybe she was in the bathroom when I came in*, she reasoned. She stared at the gorgeous female, her pulse quickening. She despised herself for letting someone have such an uncontrollable effect on her. The object of her attention caught her stare and quickly looked away.

"Hey, Harve! I thought this was a blue collar bar!" she yelled to the bartender, making certain she was loud enough for the woman to hear as well.

Harvey Barthow grunted, fatigue evident on his round face as he hurried over to her. "No trouble tonight, J.C., or out you go," he whispered in a stern tone of voice. He shook his head as he walked back to the cash register. He'd known J.C. for most of her twenty-seven years and more often than not worried about the lack of direction in her life. She was becoming more unsettled with each passing day. She wouldn't stop abusing alcohol and he was afraid she'd go somewhere else. At least here he

2455-DRON

could keep an eye on her if he saw imminent danger approaching. He shook his head as he wiped down the counter, making sure to keep an eye on her.

The woman at the end of the bar raised her head and looked long and hard at J.C. with what J.C.'s alcohol induced mind interpreted to be arrogance. J.C.'s neck muscles tightened and her jaw grew firm. No one laughed at her; she wouldn't tolerate it. She glanced at Harvey, who shot her a warning look, then threw her shoulders back and walked slowly and deliberately to the end of the bar. The woman kept her eyes focused on J.C. as she moved closer.

J.C. took a seat next to her. "What's the problem, Sam?" she demanded.

"Nothing, J.C. . . . really." Samantha's hand trembled as she brought her glass to her lips. "Can I buy you a drink?" she offered.

J.C. kept her eyes focused on Samantha's beautiful face and cringed when she saw the bruise on her left cheek that Samantha couldn't conceal, no matter how much makeup she covered it with. "I don't want a drink." She continued to stare at Samantha's cheek. "I'm sorry, Sam." Her voice softened. "It's been hell for me." She ran her hand through her tousled hair. "Please let me come back. It's been too long. I need you . . . I can't go on this way." She lowered her eyes. "You need me, too. You know you do, but you won't admit it." She reached for Samantha's hand, but Samantha quickly pulled away.

"No, J.C.," she whispered.

J.C. raised her eyes, then looked into Samantha's. "I need to feel you next to me again. I need to hold you and be held by you. You can't deny what we shared." Her voice beseeched Samantha to remember. "You want it, too."

Samantha studied J.C.'s pale, thin face. "Please, let's just forget the past. It'll only destroy us. What we had is over and we can't go back," she insisted, obviously trying to convince not only J.C., but herself.

"Why can't we? Don't you remember what we had together? I know you haven't forgotten the dreams we shared and all our good times." She softly brushed her fingertips over Samantha's bare arm, knowing that her touch affected Samantha as much as touching Samantha affected her. "I could make you feel good again. I'm the only one who will ever satisfy your passion," she said softly. "Let's go home and I'll make you forget all this pain."

Samantha fought for composure as she slowly shook her head. "There's no way it would work. I'm trying to be your friend, but that's all I can ever be to you."

"Can you forget what we meant to each other?"

"You were out of control last night. The embarrassment you caused me was totally uncalled for." Her voice was frosty.

J.C. lowered her eyes again. "What did you expect me to do? My honor was at stake."

"Your honor? For God's sake, J.C.! When are you going to grow up and face the consequences of your actions? You're a grown woman, not a teenager. If pushing me around last night helped your ego, then I feel sorry for you."

J.C. stood up. "I don't need your pity, baby." Suddenly she bent over and tenderly brushed her lips against Samantha's. "Thanks for the memories."

J.C. stormed out of the bar and into the raw, drizzly night. She pulled her jacket tighter around her thin body. A chill seeped into her bones, but it wasn't from the cold. Tears stung her eyes as she rushed across the busy intersection. She ducked into an alley and leaned heavily against the brick building. From her vantage point she could see Harve's Bar. Through teary eyes she watched couples strolling hand in hand down the street, oblivious to the rain. Her heart ached dully with envy and remorse for a love for which she had been searching all of her life and which she knew she was never meant to have.

2455-DRON

* * *

Samantha finished her drink, and then casually slid off the barstool. As she neared the door someone grabbed her arm.

"Samantha, are you all right after last night? I'm surprised to see you here tonight. I thought you'd never want to step foot in here again."

"Yes, Darcy. Just a few scratches."

"And a nice bruise," the woman observed. "You're going to file charges, aren't you?"

"No, I'm not," she stated firmly.

"Why not? Are you just going to sit back and let that dyke get away with this?"

"Don't call her that, Darcy! You don't know J.C. the way I do. Besides it was an accident. You saw what happened."

"I don't understand you, Samantha," she answered scornfully.

"Then quit trying to." Samantha scrutinized her friend. "Why are you here anyway?"

Darcy shrugged her shoulders. "I felt like getting out for awhile. I called your apartment and thought I would find you here."

"Dressed like that?" She pointed to Darcy's attire. "You look like you're going to the opera."

She chuckled. "I strive to always look my best."

"Not in this part of town. If I didn't know better, I'd think you were trying to belittle the clientele of Harve's."

"I just wanted to make certain that you're all right."

"I'm fine. I'm going to go home and settle down with a hot cup of tea and a good book."

"Sounds dull."

"Do you want to share a taxi?" Samantha offered.

Darcy looked around the smoke-filled room. "No, I think I'll stay here awhile. I hear there's a band tonight. Why don't you stay?"

She shook her head. "Not tonight."

"Because J.C.'s not here?" she asked sarcastically.

Samantha felt her face flush. "No, my decision has nothing to do with J.C.. I'm tired and just need to take it easy tonight."

Darcy laid a fleshy hand on her shoulder. "That dyke has some effect on you."

"I don't want to hear your derogatory remarks about her anymore. Is that clear?" she angrily retorted.

She held her hands up. "Okay, okay, the next time she does something to you, don't come crying to me about it. I was there and saw what that animal did to you, remember?"

"That's enough, Darcy. I've got to go." Samantha squared her shoulders then walked out of the door.

She seethed with rage as she waited for a taxi. She couldn't even begin to explain to anyone why J.C. meant so much to her. All she knew was that no matter what J.C. did she would stand by her, even though she wouldn't let J.C. know. She had to stand by her. She'd shared too much of herself, body and soul, with J.C., and J.C. would always be a part of her, even if she had to keep her distance. The only way she could help J.C. was to change the direction their bond had taken them. J.C. demanded more than she was capable of giving her, and it added insecurities to her already precarious existence. She needed to focus on her own life's desires and needed to separate herself from J.C. in order to do it, but she was wrong for forcing J.C. to believe that her drinking was the cause of all of their problems.

J.C. watched as Samantha waited for a taxi to stop. Her heart broke when Samantha stepped into the car and sped off into the night. She thought back to the first time she laid eyes on Samantha. She'd been sitting at the bar in Harve's when she walked in, her intense beauty captivating J.C.'s attention. She looked lost, out of place and so alone. It was a feeling J.C. knew well, but her curiosity caused her to wonder why this woman decided to come to Harve's of all places for a drink. Not that Harve's wasn't a friendly, homey kind of place, but this woman smelled of money and culture, and the stranger would soon realize the kind of place she happened upon wasn't what she expected. As she stole glances at

2455-DRON

the exquisite woman, her heart pounded and her palms grew sweaty. She was dressed stylishly; what a contrast J.C. made in her faded blue jeans and flannel shirt. She couldn't take her eyes off of this stranger, and found herself consumed with a burning passion that went further than a one-night stand of lust. Her knees grew weak as she envisioned holding her, stroking her, just being with her.

A sharp flash of lightning, followed by a crack of thunder, brought her out of her reverie. She'd had her chance and lost it. She had no one to blame but herself, and Samantha deserved better. J.C. regrettably remembered how Samantha had pleaded with her to stop drinking or their relationship would end, but J.C. didn't listen. She never did, and now the aftermath was hers, the loneliness that went along with it almost unbearable. But Samantha wasn't totally without blame herself, J.C. rationalized. She'd begged her for the one thing Samantha couldn't give her—security.

J.C. hunched her shoulders against the now-driving rain as she entered the street. She shivered in her thin jacket as she hurried home.

Later she sullenly sat on the worn sofa in her living room. A half bottle of whiskey sat on the dilapidated coffee table in front of her. A bold cockroach made its way through some crumbs on the table. She reached for the bottle and a glass, then in an afterthought put the glass down, sank back into the sofa, and put her feet up on the coffee table as she drank from the bottle.

She wished she could rid her mind of her tormenting thoughts and find some peace. She'd give anything for just five minutes of peace. She glared at her silent telephone. "Damn you, Sam," she muttered out loud. "Why don't you care about me?" She took another swallow from the bottle.

Hours later, J.C. groggily sat up and rubbed her eyes. She picked up the whiskey bottle and threw it across the room. "Empty!" she cried.

She stumbled into the kitchen and pulled open the cupboard doors. She knew she had another bottle somewhere; she always had another bottle. She was sure she hadn't drunk the last one.

She threw her belongings helter skelter in search of the elusive bottle. After ten minutes she slumped to the floor, enfolding her trembling body in her arms. "What's wrong with me?" she moaned as the powerful need for a drink ripped through her. "Doesn't one damned person in this fucking world care about me?" She pounded the floor with her fists, then slowly got to her feet, quickly leaning against the kitchen table to steady herself. She took a few deep breaths, grabbed her jacket, and ran out of her apartment.

Forty-five minutes later she stood outside of Samantha's apartment door. She knocked lightly. Only a few seconds passed, though to J.C. it seemed like hours. Impatiently she began beating on the door with her fists.

Samantha flung open the door. "J.C., what's the matter? It's the middle of the night," she said, her voice alarmed as she led her into the apartment. "Are you sick?"

J.C. shook her head slowly. "Please, Sam, I need to talk to you. I'm going crazy without you."

Samantha frowned as she wrapped her bathrobe tighter around herself. "I told you earlier how I feel," she said firmly. "Nothing you can say will change that."

"I remember that you also offered me a drink. I'll take it now."

Samantha let her breath out slowly. "The offer was for a drink at Harve's, not my home, but since you're here I'll give you one and only one. Then I want you to leave. What would you like?"

Her eyes shifted back and forth. "Anything."

Samantha poured some whiskey into a glass, then placed it in J.C.'s trembling hands. "Are you all right?"

J.C. nodded, desire rippling through her as Samantha's hand brushed her own. "Thanks, Sam. I owe you one the next time you're at Harve's." She gulped at the drink; its warmth quickly spread through her.

"You don't owe me anything. What's going on with you tonight? What's wrong?"

She shook her head slowly back and forth. "Sam, how can I tell you when I don't even know myself?" She took another swal-

2455-DRON

low of her drink. "I just have this terrible emptiness inside. I can't stand being away from you," she whispered in a cracked voice. "Why can't we be together again?" Her eyes pleaded with Samantha's. "It would be different this time. I promise. I'm losing my mind being away from you."

Samantha touched her arm. "J.C., you just don't take care of yourself anymore. Take a good look at yourself. Your hair hasn't been washed in days, and your clothes are torn and dirty. Look at where you live. You can do better than that dump you call home." She squeezed her arm. "But you have to want it for yourself."

"A few weeks ago I lived with you right here. That was when my life had some meaning," she said quietly. "I had a reason to live and someone to live for." She looked hopefully at Samantha.

"You know the reason I asked you to move out. I couldn't tolerate your excessive drinking any longer. I was willing to put you in a clinic and stand by you, but you refused." Her eyes grew soft. "I did want you in my life, but I couldn't stand back and watch you slowly killing yourself."

J.C. rubbed her tired eyes. "That's not entirely true. You've always had doubts about what you really want. You weren't certain if you wanted a man or me. How the hell do you think that made me feel? I not only had to worry about you falling for another woman, but also the possibility that some guy might come along and sweep you off your feet." She bit her bottom lip. "Do you know the pressure that put on me?"

"That doesn't matter now, J.C.. I'm still confused and I may be for a long time, but the one thing I'm not confused about is my need to stay away from you. I can't live with your drinking."

"But I cut down, Sam. If you let me move back in, I swear I'll stop for good. I'll go to a clinic . . . anything you want," she pleaded. "I can't go on without you!" She rapidly blinked back threatening tears.

"You're just kidding yourself, J.C.. Those are just idle promises, and I've heard the same lies over and over for years. You always cut down for a while but never entirely stop.

Whenever we argued about it and then made up, you went straight back to the bottle, forgetting the promises you made and convincing yourself that I'd forgotten them. I can't take it anymore. I've had it and in all honesty, I can't trust you."

J.C. listened to Samantha's words as disappointment rose within her. Samantha didn't understand, and there was no way she could make her understand that this separation was slashing her apart inside. She wanted to hate her, but Samantha's words rang with the truth. But she'd be damned if she'd let Samantha Wheeler think she was right. She tossed her head and hissed sarcastically, "You're a good one to talk about trust!" She grabbed the bottle of whiskey from the table. "Well, at least I can get a high class drink here." Her voice was bitter.

"Put the bottle down!" Samantha ordered. "I never should have given you a drink tonight. You've had enough!"

"I know when I've had enough, so don't tell me what I can and can't fucking do!" she shot back as she staggered into the living room and sank down into the plush sofa.

"J.C.," Samantha said in a calmer tone as she walked over to the sofa and lightly laid a hand on the younger woman's shoulder. "I know that you have problems, and I'd really like to help you, but you're going nowhere fast and that scares the hell out of me. The alcohol is just a crutch, but if you let go and learn to walk on your own you can face those demons inside of you head on. Only you can make that choice. You can be somebody, but you have to make the effort. What do you really want out of life?"

J.C. frowned, then looked into Samantha's eyes. "You," she whispered in a broken voice. "Just you." She buried her face in her hands. "I can't get over you." After a few minutes she looked up at her through moist eyes. "I'm haunted by you day and night. I feel like I'm suffocating."

Samantha swallowed hard. "J.C., you know how I feel about you. I know that I couldn't promise you forever, but I gave you what I could. Life is so uncertain, and no one knows what's going to happen from day to day. I thought you of all people lived by that rule, but

455-DRON

you kept wanting more, and when I couldn't give it to you, you ran to the bottle. Don't you see how that made me feel?"

"I wanted to be someone special to you."

"I felt responsible for bringing you so much pain, and the only way I could figure out for our individual survivals was to distance ourselves from one another. If we're both hurting then how can this union be good? I don't know who I am anymore. I do know, though, that the love we shared was very special, different from anything I'd ever experienced, and I'll never be sorry that it happened. I just need to figure out what I really want for my life, just as you do. "

"I know what I want. You. I will change. I'll do anything for you, Sam," she implored.

"Then put the bottle down and let me make a couple of phone calls to get you into treatment right now tonight."

"In the morning," J.C. said as her eyes searched Samantha's. "Let me just have this one night alone with you first."

Samantha shook her head emphatically. "Dammit, J.C. This is what I'm talking about. This is just a game to you. In the morning there'll be another excuse. You can't put anyone before that bottle. It's the only thing you truly love and someday it'll kill you. It's all ready turning on you. You're not worth anything when you're drinking, but you can't see that, can you?" she asked angrily. "You've lost everything, including me, because of it, but that still doesn't compute with you. You'll end up drinking yourself to death some day and I don't want to be around to see it!"

"Then please help me, Sam. Just leave me alone about my drinking and things will be okay. I told you I'm working on it, but I have to do it myself!" she pleaded.

"You haven't heard a word I've said!" Samantha threw her hands in the air. "Unless you admit that you have a problem, there is no one who can help you. And until you sober up, I don't want you around me. I mean it this time." Her voice was firm. "I won't take it anymore! No matter who you see me with, it's my personal business. If there is any harassment from you in any way, shape, or form, I won't hesitate to have you arrested!" She paused for a moment. "It makes me sick to my stomach to look at you and I certainly don't want to be seen in public with you looking the way you do now!"

J.C. rapidly blinked back tears, and then her eyes flashed heatedly. "So, you don't want me around?" Her voice quivered as she stood up. "Who needs you anyway, Samantha Wheeler? Do you really think you're God's gift to me? Or is this just another way to flaunt your stinking money in my face? Do you get your kicks coming to my side of town offering a world you never intend to really share? You play people and when you're finished just toss them aside like garbage. But why should you care? Your money can buy you anyone. I was always good enough in the sack, but not good enough to meet your high society friends. I'm too far below your social standing."

"J.C., you know that I've never thought I was better than anyone. But I do know that I'm the only real friend you have besides Harve. I just want you to recognize your problem and do something about it, because I do care about what happens to you. If you can't understand that, then you're even sicker than I thought."

J.C. grabbed Samantha's arm. "I'm not sick, just lonely," she said.

Samantha pushed J.C.'s hand from her arm. "Go back to your cockroach infested dump! You don't deserve any better!"

J.C. squinted as she staggered away from her. "You and I shared so much. You can't forget all those nights. Why are you treating me like this now?" she asked in a broken voice. "Why, Samantha? Don't you remember when you told me you loved me? Don't you remember the long talks when we first met and I helped you get through your pain?"

"I'm sick and tired of hiding from you whenever you get into one of your drunken rages. Or do you get some kind of satisfaction from acting tough? That is so immature! Why don't you start pushing me around right now? I'll even make it easy for you; I won't try to defend myself. Come on!" she taunted. "Let's prove how tough you are. Come on, shove me like you did last night, smart ass!" She pointed to the bruise on her cheek. "Oh, I know it was an accident. You were trying to get away from me, but instead of walking past me I happened to be in your way so you shoved me, not caring that I would be hurt in the process."

"God, Samantha, it really was an accident and you know it. I was trying to get out of there as quickly as I could. I never meant to push you. I just had to get out of there." Her eyes searched Samantha's for understanding. "I wasn't even paying attention to where I was going."

"I don't believe you."

J.C. struggled for words, but none would come. At least not any that would make any sense to Samantha or convince her otherwise. She felt hollow inside. She was well acquainted with the feeling of loneliness, but this was different. This emptiness swallowed up her very soul. She'd gone too far this time and she knew it. In the past Samantha had always taken her back, but she was different tonight. J.C. couldn't penetrate the steel barrier Samantha had placed between them. She would never find the love she had shared with Samantha with anyone else, and Samantha wouldn't either even though she assumed Samantha would probably try. She wouldn't. There had been something almost magical between them and no one could ever take Samantha's place. "I love you, Samantha. I've always loved you. You're all I have," she said in a drained voice. "I'm sorry about last night. I couldn't bear seeing you with someone else the way we used to be together; it looked like you and Darcy were more than friends to me. I snapped, but I didn't mean for you to get hurt."

Samantha ignored her words and stood firmly with hands on hips, facing her. "I want you to leave now, J.C. It's late and I need to get some sleep. Some of us have work to do in the morning."

J.C. lowered her eyes. "Could I please just stay here for tonight? I'll sleep on the couch." She ran her hand through her hair. "I don't want to be alone tonight. Please?" she begged.

"No, you'd end up trying to share my bed." She walked to the door with J.C. reluctantly following her. "When you decide to clean up your act, then maybe we can be friends. But for now, I don't care to see you anymore. Please leave!" She flung the door open.

"But . . ." She swallowed hard, hoping Samantha would change her mind.

"There's nothing more to say."

"Please. You don't know what you're saying. You can't forget what we've shared. Give me one night and I'll make you forget the past few weeks. It'll be good again, like in the beginning."

"I said I want you out of here right now!" Her voice became cold and forceful.

J.C. partially closed the door, then put a trembling hand on Samantha's arm. "I'm scared."

Samantha avoided her eyes. "Here take this with you . . . it'll give you all the courage you need. It always has!" She thrust the whiskey bottle at J.C. "Now get your ass out of here!"

"I'm really sorry, Sam. I never wanted to hurt you." Her eyes brimmed with tears. "I promise never to bother you again if that's what you really want." She looked at her for a long minute. "But just remember that I'll always love you." She looked deeply into Samantha's eyes.

Samantha glanced at her quickly, disengaging herself from J.C.'s eyes, but said nothing.

J.C. slowly walked out into the hall. She turned and looked pleadingly once again into Samantha's eyes. Then, heartbroken, she watched as Samantha silently closed the door. She took a deep breath, trying to regain her composure and at the same time looking down at the bottle clutched tightly in her hands. She raised it to her lips. "Here's to courage," she muttered. Her thoughts ran deep without making any real sense, and the terrible feeling of aloneness enveloped her. She no longer could deny the truth about herself. Samantha Wheeler was the best thing that had ever happened to her, and now it was over. She blew it and had no one to blame but herself. Knowing that it was her fault tortured her because she didn't know how to fix it. She'd used all the wiles that had worked in the past, but this time Samantha wouldn't be swayed.

2455-DRON

She could read nothing in those beautiful eyes, and a pain like death seared through her heart.

But still a spark buried deep within her refused to accept the finality of what they had once shared. They'd become almost like one—body, mind, and soul—and went too deep to be denied, no matter what Samantha said. She would never be convinced that Samantha didn't love her anymore. She couldn't end it and not feel something. She would win her back, and this time Samantha would know once and for all what she truly desired, what she'd really known all along, and there would be no more second-guessing.

J.C. knew what she had to do. She would get help for her drinking, but she would do it on her own. That would prove to Samantha that she was serious about wanting to spend the rest of her life with her. Everything would be all right again.

She was tired. She needed to go home and get some sleep. Then first thing when she woke up, she would sign herself into a clinic. She smiled as she thought how surprised and pleased Samantha would be.

* * *

Samantha leaned against the closed door, despising herself yet at the same time knowing she had no other alternative. She hated saying the cruel things she had to J.C., but she had to try to knock some sense into her. The pain in J.C.'s eyes had gone straight to her heart and she had ached to pull J.C. into her arms, but she couldn't allow J.C. to play on her sympathy any longer. She cared too much for her.

CHAPTER TWO

J.C. slowly opened her eyes, then quickly closed them against the bright light shining directly above her.

"Get up, Markin! Your attorney would like to see you now!" The voice was crisp and sharp.

J.C. started to raise her head, but a sharp pain jabbed her between the eyes forcing her to lie back down. "What the . . . ?" she muttered as she put her hand to her temple and felt a bandage wrapped around her head. "What happened to me?" she asked the woman. "Where the fuck am I? What's going on?"

"Come on this way," she said, taking J.C.'s arm and lead her down a corridor. She stopped before a room and opened the door. "Right here." She closed the door, then locked it.

J.C. slowly sat down, grimacing with pain. Her hands shook and her body desperately craved a drink. "What can I do for you?" Her tone was sarcastic as she peered at the stranger.

"More to the point is what I can do for you," he answered, calmly observing her.

J.C. sniffed. She reeked of stale whiskey and cigarettes. She looked down at her dirty jeans, then back up at the visitor. "You can get me a drink for starters."

The attorney laughed. "I think you've had all you're going to for awhile." He sat in a chair next to her, and then opened his briefcase, removing a file. "Allow me to introduce myself. I'm Ted Jamison."

"Well, Ted Jamison, I don't recall asking to see an attorney or anyone else, for that matter. I'd just like to know how the hell I ended up here."

2455-DRON

"Look, Miss Markin, you're in serious trouble. I've been appointed to represent you. It's your decision whether you choose to cooperate with me. But if I'm to defend you, I must demand your total cooperation," he said firmly.

"I can't cooperate when I don't know what's going on, now can I?" she asked with the same sarcasm.

He looked into her eyes. "What do you remember about last night?"

She nervously chewed on a fingernail, then shrugged. "About 8:00 I went to Harve's Bar and had a few drinks. Then I went home and to bed. The next thing I know, I wake up in here. Is this some kind of a joke?"

He cocked an eyebrow as he scribbled notes. "What does J.C. stand for?"

"Just J.C., that's all"

"I want to know what your initials stand for." He tapped his pen on the table.

"I don't see what my name has to do with anything," she answered. "Everybody calls me J.C.."

"If you don't want to tell me, then I can find out easily enough, Joyce Carol," he said with a smile.

She rolled her eyes. "If you already knew, then why the hassle?"

"I just wanted to see if I'm going to have your cooperation."

She shook her head. "Okay, you've got it, but now you know why I just use my initials." She grew serious. "Do you know what happened to my head? Was I in an accident or something?"

"You don't remember anything after you returned home from Harve's Bar last night?" he asked, surprised.

She frowned and racked her brain trying to remember anything unusual about last night. "No, I don't." She squinted at him. Even through her cloudy eyes she could see that he was rugged and good-looking, with a deep tan and muscles rippling beneath his suit.

"I believe you, J.C.," he said in a softer tone of voice. "As for your head, I don't know how that happened. You needed several stitches to close the wound. You don't remember that either, I take it?"

"No. Maybe a drink would jog my memory. Why am I here?"

He stared carefully at her for a moment. "I've got some bad news for you, J.C.," he finally said.

The tone of his voice frightened her. "What?"

"You've been charged with murder," he said.

She shook her head back and forth. "No way! I don't believe you! I couldn't kill anyone!" she shrieked. "What is this some kind of a sick joke? If it is, I'm not laughing!"

"I'm sorry, J.C., but the police have proof that you were at the scene of the crime."

"Crime? What crime?" she cried as he continued to scrutinize her. She swallowed hard. "Who am I supposed to have killed?" she asked hoarsely.

"Harvey Barthow."

Her eyes grew wide as shock overtook her. "Harve," she choked. "He's my friend . . . he's like a father to me." Her lips quivered. "No, I don't believe you! I love Harve." She felt like someone had plunged a knife into her heart. "No way. This is a fucking sick joke!"

"I'm not accusing you, J.C., but at approximately three o'clock this morning, you were observed outside of Mr. Barthow's apartment pounding on his door. Somehow, you forced your way inside, and twenty minutes later, you were observed exiting the apartment with a bottle in your hand. When the police arrived at the scene, Harvey Barthow was found with several stab wounds, slumped over in a kitchen chair."

J.C. continued to shake her head. "I don't believe any of this. I couldn't have done it, Mr. Jamison! Someone's trying to frame me," she sobbed. "Who claims to have seen me at Harve's?"

"We'll discuss all of that later. First, we've got to get you cleaned up."

"That witness is a liar!" She began to shake violently.

2455-DRON

"Listen to me, J.C.," he said softly. "I believe you, but I can't deny the fact that you were at his apartment."

"Forget it," she mumbled.

He looked questioningly at her. "What do you mean? You're entitled to a fair trial and it is my duty to see that you get one. It's my job to defend you to the best of my ability, but unless you're straight with me, I can't defend you."

"Look, I'm tired and I can't think right now." She rested her head in her hands. "I need a drink." She looked into his eyes. "Will you please get me one?" she pleaded.

"You know I can't do that."

She squeezed her eyes tightly shut. "I figured as much."

"Think about last night, J.C. Maybe something will come to you." He stood up. "I'll see if I can arrange bail at a later date."

J.C. was bewildered. "I didn't do it." She jumped to her feet. "You've got to believe me. I swear to you I didn't kill Harve!"

He furrowed his forehead. "I think you'd better ask yourself some serious questions about your drinking habits. I'm going to request that you undergo an alcohol detoxification treatment program as soon as possible. Will you cooperate?"

She nodded. "I didn't do it," she answered in a weak voice.

He picked up his briefcase. "I have another appointment now, but I'll be in touch with you. If you remember anything, no matter how seemingly irrelevant, please let me know as soon as possible."

"Sure," she answered numbly.

The guard escorted J.C. back to her cell, then locked the door behind her. J.C. watched as she sauntered down the corridor, whistling a popular tune

J.C. paced the small cell floor, trying to make sense out of everything. For the first time in her life, she was terrified. Her world was crashing down around her and there was nothing she could do about it. An icy blackness gripped her heart. Why couldn't she remember what had happened last night? She did remember one thing, though, and that was going to Samantha's. She wondered if she should have told Mr. Jamison, but she didn't want to drag Samantha into this mess. Going to Samantha's was the last thing she did remember about last night. Her recollection of that visit was still fresh in her mind and it tormented her. No matter what she'd had to drink, it still didn't erase that memory, but she couldn't think about it right now. Maybe her thoughts would be clearer later, and she would remember something else about last night. She couldn't think straight right now. All she knew was that Harve was dead. She couldn't imagine life without him. Tears poured from her eyes and streamed down her face. She threw herself onto her cot and let the tears flow freely.

* * *

Ted Jamison hurried to his car. The vacant look in his new client's eyes haunted him. This case would be difficult, but he believed that J.C. Markin was telling him the truth. There was something about those penetrating, dark eyes. He thought how appropriate the expression, "The eyes are the windows to the soul." In J.C.'s case he sensed this was the truth. He wondered what secrets she harbored. Were they so painful that she used alcohol, and God knew what else, to block the pain? She was so thin, and her pale complexion made him wonder when she last had a decent meal. But beneath her rough exterior there was something about her that he liked. He couldn't put his finger on it, but he liked her. His intellectual instincts told him that she honestly had no recollection of last night, and it would be up to him to prove her innocence. Now he had to find out how and why she'd ended up at Harvey Barthow's apartment.

* * *

Samantha stepped out of the shower and walked into her bedroom, deciding what to wear to the office when the doorbell sounded. "Not now," she muttered. It would be J.C. She'd have to tell the doorman not to let her up any more. That would put an end to it. Once J.C. proved to her that she was clean, she'd welcome her back with open arms, but not now. She didn't have the time or the energy for another encounter, especially after last night. "You just won't give up," she said angrily as she hurried to the door and flung it open.

"Oh, it's you."

"Well, good morning to you, too," Darcy said with a touch of annoyance in her voice.

"What did I do to deserve such an early morning visit from you?" Samantha wrapped her towel tighter around her waist. "It isn't noon yet."

Darcy's eyes gave her the once-over. "You mean you haven't heard?"

"Heard what?"

"I thought she would've called you."

"Look, I don't know what you're talking about and I don't have the time to play games," she snapped. "I've got to be at the factory by ten. There's some problem with the new line."

Darcy pushed past her and made her way into the apartment. "I think you'd better sit down, Samantha. I have some extremely painful news for you." She adjusted the collar of her jacket as she seated herself on the sofa.

Samantha studied her expression. "I don't have time for this now. Maybe we can get together for a late lunch."

Darcy slowly let her breath out. "Samantha, something terrible has happened and you need to know."

Samantha's heart began to pound. "Darcy, please tell me what's happened."

She grabbed Samantha's hands. "Harvey Barthow was murdered early this morning," she said quietly.

Samantha's eyes widened, and her hand flew to her mouth. "I don't believe it. J.C. must be going through hell. Harvey meant the world to her. What happened, Darcy?"

She shrugged. "I warned you about her. You know I told you over and over she was bad news."

"Quit talking in riddles, dammit! Can't you, for once, show some compassion for J.C.?"

"Do you think she showed any for Harvey?" Her eyes grew cold.

"What the hell are you talking about?" She searched Darcy's eyes. "Oh, no! You don't think J.C. had something to do with it, do you?"

She raised her eyebrows. "She's the prime suspect."

Samantha shook her head back and forth. "I don't believe it. She couldn't have done it. I need to talk to her!" she cried.

Darcy sneered. "Listen to yourself, Samantha! Harve is dead and all you can think about is J.C."

"You don't understand, Darcy," Samantha said quietly. "I know a part of J.C. that no one else does. There's a sweet, gentle, loving side that she rarely shows to anyone. She's had a hard life and never had things come easily as we did."

"Samantha, you aren't listening to reason. You had your fling with her and now it's over," she said. "A man is dead, for God's sake, but you feel sorry for his murderer!" She threw her hands up. "I give up on you. You're hopeless. I hope the dyke rots in prison for the rest of her miserable life!"

"Don't call her that!" Her eyes flashed angrily. "And don't you ever try to demean my relationship with her. What she gave me is something you'll never understand."

"I pity you." She stood up and glanced at her wristwatch. "I just stopped by to give you the news. I've got some errands to run."

Samantha followed her and opened the door. Darcy laid a hand on Samantha's trembling shoulder.

"Stay away from her, Samantha," she warned. "What you had with her is over. You can't help her anymore."

Samantha quietly closed the door behind Darcy, then walked back into her living room. She paced the floor for a few minutes before wearily sinking into a chair. She felt so cold and lost. Her mind was traumatized by Darcy's news. She knew how outraged

J.C. could become when she was provoked, but she also knew the tender, sweeter side of her. There was no way in hell anyone could ever convince her that J.C. was capable of murder. She had to find out the truth.

She'd had many stormy conflicts in the past with J.C., but J.C. had never shown any physical violence towards her or anyone else, and in her heart she knew that what had happened the other night truly was an accident. J.C. had seen her talking closely to Darcy, and even though she and J.C. were no longer a couple, J.C.'s jealousy came through. Samantha wanted to explain to J.C. that she'd misinterpreted the encounter, but even if she hadn't, it was over between them. J.C. pushed past her, not knowing that Samantha had fallen. But when J.C. realized what had happened and rushed back over to help, Samantha lashed out at her, falsely accusing her of causing her to fall. She should have told her last night that she knew it was an accident, but she was at the end of her rope and thought maybe J.C. would get help if she truly believed she'd done it intentionally. Now she wished she would've let her spend the night. She'd never forget the tormented look in those lost and lonely eyes for as long as she lived.

She had tried many times to convince J.C. how special their relationship was, but J.C. never quite believed that Samantha would stay loyal to her. J.C. was the only woman Samantha had ever slept with, and it was something that neither of them had planned to happen. It left Samantha confused about whom she really was and what sex she truly wanted to be with. J.C. brought out the wild side of her that had been suppressed all of her life. Her cultured breeding would never let her even imagine the things that J.C. had actually done. She had no doubts when J.C. pledged her devotion to her that J.C.'s love was anything but absolute. J.C. had shown her that it was the most natural thing in the world, but a part of her still needed to be positive that she no longer desired to be with a man. The more she tried to explain her feelings to J.C., the more love and attention J.C. lavished on her, as though trying to convince her. Her passion knew no bounds, but it only made Samantha feel more bewildered than ever. She didn't know herself anymore and it frightened her.

She wished she could turn back time, but she would never be regretful for her relationship with J.C. J.C. had been such a compassionate and patient teacher, showing her how to let go of all her inhibitions and fully experience every depth of her sexuality. She had been frightened and confused after their first time together, but J.C. had tenderly held her all through the night, soothing her worries away. Everything had seemed so pure and natural with J.C. that Samantha had soon found herself returning J.C.'s love with the same passion J.C. gave to her. Touching and exploring her lover's body came without reflection; she loved the firmness of J.C.'s small breasts and her full, sensuous lips. J.C. never tired of satisfying her every desire in and out of bed, but Samantha had put one condition on her.

Their love had to be kept secret. To the world they were just friends, but in the still of the night they fervently explored one another's bodies. She hadn't understood how intensely her confusion had affected J.C., but she had noticed the increase in her drinking. She wished now that she had paid closer attention to J.C.'s needs. J.C. knew and accepted her own sexual preference and couldn't fully understand how one could not know her true choice. Maybe J.C. had thought she was playing games or worse yet, poking fun at her.

She'd always known that J.C. was a drinker, but never realized that the drinking was a mask for all the hurts she had suffered in the past. J.C. could never seem to bring herself to share her grief with Samantha, no matter how many times Samantha tried to get her to open up. It was only when J.C.'s drinking became uncontrollable that Samantha realized she needed professional help. Her anger and restlessness frightened her, even though J.C. had never acted out her anger on anyone. Just the same, she often wondered if J.C. would someday reach the point that she would lose all control.

A tear fell from Samantha's eye. She ached to see J.C. and comfort her. She needed to let her know how much she cared.

* * *

J.C. shielded her eyes against the harsh overhead light. The more she tried to cover her eyes, the brighter the light seemed to become. The pain rippling through her body was almost unbearable with her insides all mashed together. She was dying and no one cared; she was left here in this stinking cell lying in her own vomit, and this was all she had to show for her life. She tried to clear her mind, but the more she tried the more fogged it became. This pain was like nothing she'd ever felt before as she drifted in and out of reality. When her dinner tray came, she frantically searched it, hoping for something stronger than a carton of milk but knowing nothing would be there. She needed a drink—anything, just something to take away this horrendous pain. She couldn't think straight; a drink would clear her mind. "Please!" she moaned. Sweat trickled from her brow as she rolled to her side on the cot, wrapping herself tightly in her arms. "I'm losing my fucking mind!" she screamed. She writhed in pain for a few minutes, then jumped from the cot and ran to the bars. She pounded on them, beating them until her knuckles were bloody, then slumped to the floor as screams tore from her and echoed through the corridor.

She watched a small group making their way toward her. They opened the cell door, and she crawled toward it. Hands reached out to her, so many hands it made her dizzy. She tried to slap them away. She kicked and punched at them; they threw her on her back and put her arms and legs in restraints. "No!" she screamed as their snake-like fingers probed her. She wouldn't look at them. She turned her face to the bare wall, only now it wasn't bare. Bugs were swarming all over it. The bugs looked at her with angry expressions on their faces as they slowly marched toward her. She had to stop them or soon they would be all over her. She screamed again, but no one paid any attention to her as they continued examining every orifice on her. One of the bugs reached her, and when she gazed into its eyes it seemed to come out of its body and evolve into a snake. It slithered under her. She tried to warn the others, but they couldn't seem to hear her. "Oh, God!" she screamed, as the bugs covered her arms and legs, their tiny mouths opening to devour her.

* * *

Samantha hurried into Ted Jamison's office. "I'm sorry, I'm late," she apologized.

He looked up from the file he'd been poring over. "That's quite all right, Miss Wheeler." He removed his reading glasses and lay them on the cluttered desk. "What can I do for you?"

"J.C. Markin. I'm a friend of hers and I was told that you've been assigned to her case."

"That's correct." He studied the woman's attire. She was stylishly outfitted in a navy blue dress, which clung to her every curve. Her jewelry wasn't the costume type he was accustomed to seeing on his clients, but the genuine article. He frowned. "Do you have some information for me?"

"No, but I was hoping that bail would be arranged for J.C. Money is no object," she offered.

"I don't think bail will even be considered in J.C.'s case." He carefully eyed her.

"Why?"

He leaned back in his chair. "J.C. isn't exactly the sort of person the state can be convinced won't jump bail." He folded his hands. "She has nothing to prevent her from running—no family ties, job, boyfriend. We need to face facts here. She would be considered a very high-risk case."

"Isn't there something we can do?" Samantha pleaded. "What if I agree to put up the bail on the condition that J.C. stay with me? My reputation in this city is impeccable."

"I still don't think the judge will buy it."

"Can't we at least try?"

He looked into her bright blue eyes, wondering why she would stake her reputation to help his client. "Have you known her long?"

"For several years," she answered. "And I know that she did not murder Harvey Barthow," she firmly stated.

"How can you be so sure?"

"I know J.C. better than anyone. She loved Harvey. He was like a father to her."

He frowned. "I'll see what I can do." When he saw the relief flood her face, he quickly added, "Now don't get your hopes up. Judge Ryan is tough. And we have to remember the prosecution. The state may convince him that it isn't wise to let her out. We don't know all the evidence the state has against her."

"I'll take that chance, Mr. Jamison." She smiled brightly.

"Okay, then. I'll be in touch with you as soon as I can get a hearing."

* * *

"You've barely touched your dinner, Samantha. What's wrong?"

Samantha glanced at Darcy. "I'm not very hungry."

Darcy set her fork down, looking angrily at her friend. "What's with you, Samantha? J.C. Markin is a loser and it's time you accepted it. She's brought nothing but pain and suffering to you."

"No," Samantha interrupted. "No one will ever know her the way I do. I can't stand by and watch her suffer. I'll go to my grave knowing that she's innocent!"

Darcy threw her hands up in exasperation. "I don't know what to say to convince you. We've been friends for most of our lives and I swear to God, I've never seen you like this before."

"I don't know what to do." She looked pleadingly at Darcy.

"I can't offer any sympathy, you know that," she answered firmly. "Don't ask me to be a hypocrite."

She nodded. "But she never did anything to you." She searched the woman's eyes.

Darcy avoided her penetrating look. "If you've finished, we may as well leave."

"Yes," Samantha said quietly.

Darcy grabbed her arm. "Hey, I've got an idea. Why don't you spend the night with me?"

Samantha shook her head. "No. I need to do some thinking."

"Suit yourself, but if you change your mind, the invitation is always open." She frowned. "You need to be around people, Samantha."

"Thank you for your concern, but I'll be fine."

After Darcy dropped her off Samantha hurried into her apartment and over to the answering machine. No messages awaited her. With a heavy heart she walked into the kitchen and fixed a cup of tea. She took it to her desk, where a framed photograph of J.C. greeted her. She smiled when she recalled the resistance J.C. had put up when she had insisted on the picture. She picked up the photo and held it tightly against her chest, cherishing the memories of the good times they shared. She couldn't let go of J.C., but she had to. If only J.C. could know how much she really did love her.

The phone rang but, thinking it was Darcy, she didn't pick it up. She listened to her cheerful greeting, then heard Ted Jamison's voice. She quickly grabbed the receiver. "Hello."

"Miss Wheeler?"

"Yes, this is Samantha Wheeler. Do you have news about J.C.?" she hopefully asked.

"Yes, Judge Ryan has agreed to see you to discuss bail, but I wouldn't get your hopes up," he warned.

She smiled. "I know I can win him over," she said confidently. "When can I see J.C.?"

"She's been taken to the hospital."

"Oh my God! What's happened to her?" she cried.

"Calm down. She's going through alcohol withdrawal and she needed some medical treatment to help her through it."

"Does she know that I've been trying to see her?"

"No, she hasn't been in any condition to fully understand anything. It's going to take a few weeks for her treatment, and then Judge Ryan will evaluate her progress. If he likes what he sees, then he will meet with you."

"When will I know?" she asked.

"I'll be in touch," he promised.

Samantha hung up the telephone, then walked into the spare bedroom to prepare it for J.C. The stakes were stacked against J.C. being released on bail, but making up the room for her made her feel that somehow she could turn the odds in J.C.'s favor.

CHAPTER THREE

J.C., suspiciously peering at the others surrounding the large table, sipped at her coffee. One by one everyone gave his or her first name and said, "I'm an alcoholic". *What a crock*, she thought. When it was her turn, she looked defiantly at the leader but said nothing.

"Would you like to tell us your name?" he asked softly.

She leaned back in her chair, eyeing him.

"We've all been there. We're your friends. We just want to help," he coaxed.

"Yeah, sure," she snarled, grasping the cup tighter in her hands.

"How long since you've had a drink?" he asked.

She shrugged her shoulders.

"Well, let me tell you a little bit about myself. My name is Hank and I'm an alcoholic."

She rolled her eyes. "I didn't ask and I don't care."

"We all want to help you." He waited for a few seconds, and when she didn't respond continued, "All of us around this table are alcoholics and everyone of us has a different story to tell. Maybe some are worse than others, but we've all been there. And our drinking is the reason we're in jail." He continued to look at her as he talked. "I'm in here for vehicular manslaughter." He threw his hands in the air. "Sure, I was angry and thought the whole world was against me, but it was only when I admitted that alcohol was at the core of my screwed up life that I could finally do something about it. It's not easy, but with all of us here banding together, we can lean on each other. We're family." He smiled cheerfully. "And those who have been released never forget where they've been. Most

2455-DRON

come back to the meetings here because they want others to know they've been where you are today."

J.C. set the cup on the table. "What's your name? I forgot."

"Hank," he smiled. "What's yours?"

"J.C."

"Hi, J.C."

"Hi, J.C.," the others said in unison with those sitting on either side of her grabbing her hands, gently shaking them.

"Do you want to talk, J.C.?" Hank offered.

"I—I'm not too good in groups," she stuttered.

"Here you don't have to worry what you say or how you say it."

She contemplated whether she should trust these men and women. They were strangers to her. Why would they care about what happened to her? But she was lonely, and these were the only real people—besides counselors, doctors, and nurses—with whom she'd had a chance to communicate for the past several weeks. "I've been accused of something I didn't do." She searched their faces. They were all looking at her, but they weren't scornful. Instead they appeared friendly and caring. She wondered what the woman sitting next to her was in for. She looked like one of those grandmothers you saw on the commercials—round and jovial, always in the kitchen baking something. "But I can't remember." She blinked hard. "I wouldn't kill anyone."

"Were you drunk?" Hank softly asked.

She nodded.

The grandmotherly one sitting next to her put a protective arm around her. "We all have stories like yours, J.C. Alcohol robbed us of our memories, but we can change. Just give it one day at a time. It won't be easy, but we're all here to help you. You have to admit that alcohol is your enemy and not your friend."

"Do you ever crave a drink?" J.C. asked.

She laughed. "Every time something doesn't go my way. But I fight it. I remember all the pain I've brought to others and myself because of my drinking. I won't give in to it. I go to meetings or contact a friend to talk it out. If I pick up a drink, it might as well be a gun pointed at my head. I want to be in control of myself, but alcohol renders me incompetent."

J.C. lowered her eyes. "I'm so frustrated."

"Sure you are, honey, but we're your friends. Just give us a chance. Once you can admit you have a problem with alcohol, you can change. My name is Helen and I'm proud to say I'm an alcoholic."

"Proud?" J.C. asked, thinking the woman must surely have a screw loose.

"Yes, proud. It keeps me honest. When I keep first in my thoughts that I'm an alcoholic, I know that no one can make me pick up a drink, but myself. I spent years trying to blame everyone and everything for my mistakes. If I was drunk, then that was the best excuse of all, because I had to take no responsibility for my actions or the hateful things I said to others. I've hurt a lot of people through the years, but now I'm trying to undo some of the damage. All I can do is try. But if I choose to pick up a drink, then I have no one to blame for what happens but myself."

"I've hurt someone very close to me."

Helen nodded. "If you want to talk about it, we'll listen. Just take your time."

J.C. looked at the friendly, smiling faces. They appeared sincere, but could she really be certain? She swallowed hard and tried to make sense out of her jumbled thoughts.

* * *

Samantha nervously clutched her purse in her sweaty palms, observing the judge's expression as he reviewed his paperwork. Finally he peered at her from the wire-rimmed glasses perched atop his nose. "Samantha Wheeler?"

"Yes, Your Honor."

"You do understand the nature of this crime?"

"I do."

He removed his glasses, continuing to eye her. "Why do you want to do this?"

"I don't believe that Joyce Markin committed this crime."

"It's not as simple as that, Miss Wheeler. There is evidence placing her at the scene of the crime."

"Your Honor," Ted interrupted, "the defense has not been presented with any evidence that can positively identify Joyce Markin as the murderer of Harvey Barthow."

"Are you in agreement with this bail request?" he asked Stu Brewster, counselor for the prosecution.

"No, Your Honor. Joyce Markin would be a risk. We have no guarantee that she won't jump bail."

He frowned. "Is that all?"

"No, due to the nature of the crime, we feel it is in the best interest to keep her incarcerated until her trial date."

"She has been getting treatment for her alcoholism and treatment will continue," Ted stated.

"That won't stop her from skipping the country," Stu vehemently stated.

"Come on, Stu, Samantha Wheeler is staking her reputation on Joyce Markin." He looked hard at the older man. "All you have is a witness who saw her outside of Harvey Barthow's apartment building. That doesn't prove anything."

"It was enough to make her our prime suspect."

"Joyce Markin isn't a risk."

The judge leafed through the papers before him. After a few minutes, he stared at Samantha. "Miss Wheeler, convince me that releasing Joyce Markin to your custody will be in the best interest of this court."

* * *

J.C. walked back and forth in her tiny cell. Six weeks had passed, but to her most of it was a blur. She turned to her new friends when the loneliness became too much to bear. But none of them could ease the void in her that Samantha had caused. At night when the lights were turned out she relived the moments they'd spent together, then held her pillow to her face to muffle the sounds of her sobs. Samantha hadn't even bothered to visit or call. It was over between them and she had to accept that fact, but that was the difficult part. She would never be able to forget Samantha Wheeler. She'd touched her heart and soul like no other woman had ever been able to.

"Markin, your attorney is here."

J.C. turned, then smiled when she saw Ted Jamison peering into the cell. "Let him in," she said.

He took a pack of cigarettes from his pocket and offered her one. She readily accepted it.

"What's this?" she asked with a slight smile. "My final cigarette before facing the firing squad?"

He laughed as he lit the cigarette for her, then put the lighter back into his pocket. "I have some good news for you, J.C. It was quite a battle, but bail has been arranged for you."

"How much?" she asked.

"Half a million."

She laughed sarcastically. "Why not one million? I'm sure you told the judge I'll have the money by noon." She crushed out the cigarette. "I'll have to sit it out until my trial."

"Cheer up. Your bail's been taken care of."

She raised her eyebrows in surprise.

"There have been conditions put on your release, though."

"Who put up bail?"

"Samantha Wheeler. I'm here to take you to her apartment after we get you processed."

J.C.'s heart lurched at the mention of Samantha's name, but she was still bitter. "I don't want to see her."

He frowned. "Is there a problem between you two?"

She tossed her head. "I don't know."

"Level with me, J.C. It's your call," he said.

Her choice was inevitable. She finally had a chance to get out of this cell and back into the world—if only for a little while. Besides, she had to find out why Samantha would risk so much money on her if it truly were over between them. "Okay, I'll see her."

Samantha hurried to the door and flung it wide open. "J.C.!" she cried. "How are you?" She threw her arms around her, pulling her close.

"I'm fine," J.C. answered quietly, shrugging off the embrace even though she wished she could stay in the comfort of Samantha's arms. But she could never let Samantha know the effect she had on her. Not now, not after Samantha had forced her out of her life.

"Thank you, Mr. Jamison," Samantha beamed, turning to Ted.

He returned her smile. "You're quite welcome, Miss Wheeler."

"Please call me Samantha," she offered.

He nodded. "J.C. is fortunate to have you for a friend, Samantha." He turned his attention to J.C. "Remember what I told you—stay out of trouble. No bars, or your bail will be revoked. I'll be in touch."

"I know," J.C. scowled, angry for being treated like a child instead of the grown woman she was.

"Thank you again," she said, then closed the door behind him. She turned to J.C. and embraced her for a second time.

J.C. smelled the fragrance of her hair, wishing the hug meant more than a friendly gesture, but Samantha would never again embrace her that way. She yearned to hold Samantha close, enveloping her in her arms and never letting her go. She ached to feel her bare flesh next to her own once more. In her AA meetings some talked about how they were given second chances. Could she even dare hope that she'd be given one? Would Samantha once again fill her life with meaning? But she also learned that she couldn't count on anyone else to make her happy. It had to first come from within herself. When she could truly love and accept herself, then she could receive what others had to offer, but her emotions were too raw to contemplate all of this now. Her heart had been ripped wide open and she needed time to heal her raw, gaping wounds.

"You're so pale and thin, J.C. I'm going to take care of you and get you healthy once again."

J.C. wanted to graciously accept her hospitality, but she'd be damned if she'd let Samantha see her vulnerable. "Why would you want to do that?" she demanded, her dark eyes flashing angrily. "The last time I came here, if my memory serves me right, you said you didn't want me around anymore."

"Things have changed," Samantha answered in a quiet tone of voice. "Please sit down and make yourself comfortable, and I'll get us some coffee."

J.C. sat on the sofa, her eyes looking around the familiar room. Finally she focused on the well-stocked bar. She got up and walked over to it, picking up one bottle at a time and studying the familiar labels.

"Here's your coffee, J.C." Samantha's voice was sharp.

J.C., startled, slowly turned around. "Don't worry, Samantha, I wasn't going to steal any of your precious whiskey."

"I hope not."

J.C. laughed bitterly.

Samantha set the tray on the coffee table. "You can't drink, J.C. You've been doing so well these past weeks and . . ."

"And how the hell would you know how I'm doing?"

Samantha flinched at the harshness of J.C.'s voice. "I called everyday for an update on you, J.C. I was worried about you."

"Why don't you just rephrase that? You mean you called to see if I'd snap without the booze."

"No—No, I didn't."

"Hey, look! It doesn't really matter anymore; nothing does."

Samantha sighed. "To alleviate the pressure while you're here, I'm going to remove the bottles." She searched J.C.'s eyes. "I want to help you in any way that I can."

"Well, don't worry, Samantha, because I don't intend to spend much time here. And even if I did, I wouldn't drink any of your precious booze. Seeing it doesn't cause me any pressure!"

"Just the same, I'll feel better if it's not around you." She forced a tight smile. "Now, please sit down and drink your coffee. There are a few things we need to discuss." She folded her hands, then placed them in her lap.

"Don't tell me what to do! I'm not some fucking two-year-old!"

Samantha felt her face grow warm as she tried to calm the anger rising inside her. "J.C., why don't you just cut the act? You're in serious trouble and I'm trying to help you."

"Why?"

"Maybe because I'm concerned about you."

"Why should you care?" she asked angrily.

"I honestly don't know why I should care. I've asked myself that question at least a hundred times." She looked into J.C.'s eyes. "Maybe it's because I can see something in you that no one else can. There is something good and very honest under that mask, J.C. But what I do know for sure is that you shouldn't drink. But you never listen. Alcohol will be your undoing someday, but you refuse to see it. Every time you pick up a drink, you're bringing yourself closer to death. I'm watching you commit a slow and painful suicide, and it hurts me more than you will ever know. You are only using alcohol to hide from your past hurts instead of facing them head on. I'm sorry that you had such a terrible life, but it's not my fault and it's about time that you grew up and started taking responsibility for your actions."

J.C. jumped to her feet. "I don't have to listen to this bullshit! Who the fuck do you think you are to preach to me?"

"Sit your ass down!"

Samantha's tone and language caught J.C. off guard. Her jaw was set firmly as her eyes stayed focused on her. She'd never seen this side of Samantha before. She reseated herself.

"It's about time that someone laid it on the line for you. Look at yourself. Go on, take a good hard look, for God's sake! You have so much potential but refuse to do anything to better yourself. It's easier for you to blame everyone else for the misfortunes in your life instead of using a little blood, sweat, and tears to change your circumstances." She saw the pain in J.C.'s eyes that J.C. tried to conceal. It broke her heart to hurt her, but it was the only way she could get through to her.

J.C. looked up. "We used to be so close, Sam. It seems like it was years ago now." She swallowed hard. "I love you. That has never stopped for me. I don't know why you ended our relationship. I was so hurt when you never visited me in jail. I thought you didn't care. I couldn't take it when you said you didn't want to see me anymore. I don't care about anything anymore . . . especially now with Harve gone." A tear slid from her eye, making a slow descent down her cheek. "I don't know what happened that night; I wish to God I could remember, but I can't. When I came here that night I thought that maybe you would have missed me so much that you would want me back." She cleared her throat. "But I swear to you that I did not kill Harve. I know I was set up and I've been racking my brain trying to figure this out." She twisted her fingers through her hair. "I don't have any recollection of anything after I left here that night. At first I thought I was losing my mind. I just wish I could remember," she sobbed.

"You can't remember because you were drunk, J.C. If you'd take some time and try to go over the past five years of your life, you'd be shocked at how much you probably can't remember. There were countless nights when I had to practically carry you out of Harve's, then bring you home and put you to bed. I thought if I took care of you, you would stop drinking, but I was wrong. By helping you I was only hurting you more, and I couldn't continue on that way. It was destroying the both of us."

"Okay, please back off about my drinking. It's tough getting a drink in jail." She shrugged. "It doesn't matter if you believe me or not, but I've really stopped for good this time. I've been in treatment and I'm attending AA. I met some nice people there." She looked at Samantha. "You'll never believe me, and I don't care anymore if you do or not," she lied, knowing that she did want

Samantha's approval and encouragement. "Look, it's been a long day and I'm really beat. I'd better leave." She stood up.

"You can't leave."

She looked quizzically at her. "Why?"

"Didn't your attorney explain to you the conditions of your bail?"

"He told me that you posted bond and I had to see you—oh, no . . . I'd rather be back in jail than have you for my warden!"

Samantha's eyes softened. "I care about you, J.C., or I wouldn't have risked my reputation for you."

J.C.'s stomach twisted into a big knot. "So, if it wasn't for the great Samantha Wheeler and her damned money, then I would still be rotting in that cell!" she spat out. "I wish you would have just left me there! I don't need any favors from you!"

"J.C., I only did it because I care about you. Bail wasn't even considered until you went through alcohol abuse treatment. I fought for you. For God's sake, can't you forget that damned stubborn pride of yours? I was fighting for your release from day one." She shook her head in disbelief. "You need to grow up and face life. You need someone in your corner and I'm that person whether you like it or not. Take the blinders off and open your eyes for once! Who do you think you are? The indestructible J.C. doesn't need anyone! Right! You need me more than you'll ever know. You're lonely; it's eating away at you, but you won't admit it. You'll never be thankful for anything I've ever tried to do for you. All I get is a kick in the ass for my efforts! I'm fed up. I've had it! Then go. Get the hell out of here!"

"No, Sam," J.C. moaned, covering her face with her hands. "I'm so sorry," she cried.

J.C.'s shoulders heaved up and down. Samantha put her arms around J.C., holding her close and gently rocking her as a mother would rock her child. She brushed the tangled hair from J.C.'s brow.

"Sam, why won't anyone believe me?" she gulped. "Harve was like the father I never had," she said in a broken voice.

"You don't have to convince me. If I didn't believe you, I wouldn't be here now trying to help you. Are you willing to accept my help?" she asked gently.

"Yes." J.C. swiped at her eyes.

Samantha gave her a squeeze. "You must be starved. I'm going to fix you something to eat. Why don't you lie down for awhile?"

"Sounds like a good idea." She smiled through her tears. "Care to join me?" she softly asked, caressing Samantha's arm. "I am starved, but only for you." J.C.'s fingers melted into her flesh, bringing back floods of memories of those fingers and hands roaming over every inch of her bare flesh.

"We can't, J.C.. That's over for us," she said weakly.

J.C. brushed her lips over Samantha's soft cheek, then moved to her full lips. Samantha's body trembled, and a soft moan escaped her lips. "Just one more time."

Samantha pushed her away. "No, J.C.," she said breathlessly. "We can't."

"Why? You want it as much as I do, baby," she whispered as she continued to move her hands over Samantha's body. "I want you. Tell me that you want me just as much. I need to feel you next to me again . . . just this one night. Then it'll be over if that's what you really want. I promise." She lightly ran her fingertips over Samantha's breasts, feeling the quivering effect it had on her lover.

"No," Samantha moaned as she pushed her body closer instead of away from J.C.

J.C. gently laid her back on the sofa, stroking the flesh she'd ached for so long. "You are so beautiful," she murmured, removing Samantha's clothing, then her own. All of her pent up emotions washed over her like a wave as her craving for Samantha escalated and finally reached the crescendo of their union.

Afterward J.C. put an arm around Samantha, feeling the passionate woman she'd just made love to stiffen at her touch. "I'm sorry. I shouldn't have done that," she apologized.

"I could have said no."

455-DRON

"But I wouldn't let you."

Samantha squeezed her eyes tightly shut for a moment. "You knew that I needed you—that we needed each other. I did miss you, J.C." She lightly ran her fingertips over J.C.'s bare thigh. "The sensible part of me wanted to push you away, but I succumbed to my own selfish needs."

J.C. enclosed Samantha in her arms. "I only asked for one more night with you. I'll never get you out of my system, but I have to let you go. In jail I realized that I've been wrong to hold you back. You still desire men, and I have no right to deny you the right to make your own choice." She kissed Samantha's cheek. "I want you to have it all, but I can't share you, honey. I thought I could, but after being with you just now, I know that I can't. I want all of you or nothing. I need to be with you for this one night, then I'll release you to choose what you must."

"But I do want you, J.C.," Samantha protested. "I need you to touch me, hold me, love me, and make me feel alive again." Her eyes searched J.C.'s.

"It's the passion of the moment," she quietly answered. "But can you be committed just to me?"

Her eyes filled with tears. "I can't promise I won't be with a man again, but you're the only woman I want to be with."

"I know and I thank you for your honesty," J.C. whispered. "We have tonight, and it will be our last night together as lovers until you make a decision." She tenderly kissed Samantha's neck, then let her mouth expertly travel over her lover's body, trying to make this night last forever.

* * *

Ted slammed his drink down on the table. "Be reasonable, Stu! You would've done the same thing if you were in my place."

"Face it, Ted. You're the new kid on the block and I think you're biting off more than you can chew," Brewster stated matter-of-factly.

"I believe that my client is innocent. There is no concrete evidence to convict her."

"You're not facing facts, Ted. There was enough evidence for the grand jury to indict her. And there is a witness."

"But the witness didn't see any crime taking place. The coroner's report put the time of death one hour before J.C. was seen entering the building."

"What are you going to use in her defense, Ted? She could've been returning to the scene of the crime. You've got yourself a difficult case. Get her to plead guilty and we'll work something out."

Ted thoughtfully scratched his chin as he picked his drink back up. "I believe the woman was framed. I know it doesn't sound like much, but there is an air of innocence about her."

"Innocence!" Stu roared. "You've seen her record and you're going to defend her on grounds of her character?" He shifted his heavy frame in his chair.

Ted shook his head as he looked at his older and more seasoned opponent. Nothing he could say would convince a man of Stu Brewster's caliber of J.C.'s innocence. Men like Brewster went after facts, not hunches. "I've got to do it my way, Stu. I may be wrong, and God damn me if I am, but in any event Joyce Markin won't be any worse off for it."

He exhaled loudly. "I wish you luck, Ted, because when I get little Miss Markin on the stand, she'd better have a solid alibi. I'm going to tear her to shreds." He glanced at his watch. "Well, I'd better be off. The wife's invited a few friends for dinner and I'll catch hell if I'm late."

"That's why I'm a confirmed bachelor," Ted answered with a wink. Stu slapped him on the back.

Ted watched Stu make his way to the exit, then ordered another scotch and water. Stu would keep putting pressure on him to convince J.C. to plead guilty, but he still couldn't get rid of the gut feeling that J.C. was innocent. He believed it with every thread of his being, but proving it would be one of the most difficult challenges he'd ever encountered in his career. Samantha Wheeler was convinced of her friend's innocence. He was curious about the friendship the two women shared and what had brought them together. They came from two different worlds and were complete opposites as far as he could see.

His mind wandered to thoughts of Samantha. On their first meeting, he'd been immediately struck with her intense beauty and soft manners and speech. He had expected her to be arrogant as most wealthy young women he'd met tended to be, but instead she was warm and friendly toward him, and her deep concern for her friend impressed him. He'd been embarrassed for his preconceived expectations of her, preparing himself for an unbearable meeting. But when he first set eyes on her he felt comfortable and at ease in her company, and found himself looking forward to their next meeting.

* * *

"Were you expecting anyone, Sam?" J.C. asked as the ringing of the doorbell persisted.

"No. I'll get rid of whoever it is, so don't worry." She smiled reassuringly.

Samantha opened the door a crack and peered out into the hall. "I'm sorry, Darcy, but I'm extremely busy today. You should've called first," she said coolly.

"I'll only take a few minutes of your time," Darcy said, pushing her way past Samantha. "Well, well, look who's here," she said sarcastically as she made her way into the living room. "I heard you were out on bail, and I had a hunch you would end up here."

"Please leave, Darcy," Samantha said firmly.

"I want to ask your little friend a few questions first." She stood menacingly in front of J.C., twisting a string of pearls that hung loosely around her neck. J.C. shot her a look of disgust.

"I don't intend to answer any of your questions, Darcy."

The older woman whirled around and faced Samantha. "Everyone's talking about you, Samantha. They can't understand why you would bail this murderer out of jail and then invite her to stay in your home. I'm trying to defend your reputation, for God's sake!"

"That's enough, Darcy! I don't care what anyone thinks anymore! Just get out and leave us alone!"

Darcy's words pierced J.C. She couldn't let Samantha risk her reputation for her. "She's right, Sam. Don't jeopardize your future for me. This was a mistake—I shouldn't be here."

"No, she's not right. She's nothing but a troublemaker!" She shook with anger. "I've been waiting a long time to tell you what I really think of you, Darcy Sebastion."

"Face the truth, Samantha. It's about time you cleared the cobwebs out of your head. She's nothing but a drunk. That's not your style," she answered calmly. "Until this phase you're going through runs its course, if you want a woman, I know a couple of lesbians who are in our social class."

Samantha's cheeks flamed. "Don't be absurd!"

Darcy looked antagonizingly at J.C. "Take a good hard look at her. She's nothing but filthy trash! She's beneath you," she taunted. "Why are you shaking, J.C.? Thinking about how good a double shot of whiskey would taste right about now? Just think, you could drink yourself into oblivion and not be accountable for anything you say or do." She leered at her. "You're trapped this time, hot shot! You can't get out of this one. Guilt is written all over your face!"

J.C. held back the words that threatened to spill out. That was what Darcy really wanted, for her to lose control. But she would never give her the satisfaction—not this time, not ever again.

"That's enough! Get out!" Samantha ordered, roughly grabbing Darcy's arm.

"Okay, I'm leaving." She chuckled to herself. "I'm just trying to protect you, Samantha, but since you don't want my help, I'll

455-DRON

save it for court. Your dyke is the one with blood on her hands, not me. Just remember who the enemy is here."

"Court? What are you talking about, Darcy?" Samantha demanded.

"We'll all be petitioned. They need character references for your dear friend, and I'm certain that everyone who's ever known her will have quite a story to tell about your precious lover. But the best part will be when they get to her sordid love life."

"I don't believe you, Darcy."

"I don't care if you do or do not, Samantha." She flashed J.C. a bright smile. "See you in court."

Samantha slammed the door with such a force that a picture rattled on the wall. "The nerve of that woman!" She put an arm protectively around J.C. "Don't let her upset you."

"I don't want to hurt you anymore or cause you any more pain," she said quietly. "No one has ever known about us, except Darcy and the crowd at Harve's, and you know they would never say anything. I've always kept us a secret like you wanted, but I think under the circumstances I shouldn't stay here now. You've got to think about your reputation. I'll call Mr. Jamison and await my trial in jail."

Samantha grabbed her hand. "No, you won't. It's no one's business what I do in my private life. I know I asked you to keep our relationship secret, but I'm tired of hiding. If it comes out in court, then I'll face the consequences." She squeezed her hand tightly. "I think you should tell Mr. Jamison that you were here the night of Harvey's murder, and about us."

"I can't," she protested.

"I think you need to. It might shed some light on your case."

She sighed. "I don't know . . . I'll think about it. I'm tired."

"Why don't you lie down, and I'll be in later."

Her eyes clouded. "No, Sam, no more. Last night was the last. I told you that I have to let you go. I know that I'd be happy spending the rest of my life with only you, but you can't give me that same commitment. If the day ever comes when you can, then you know where I'll be—waiting for you with open arms."

"J.C., I was wrong in asking you to move out." She wrung her hands. "I should've addressed your alcohol problem differently."

"No, you did what you had to do. But I couldn't deal with the uncertainty of our relationship."

"J.C., I wish I could tell you what you want to hear, but I can't. Now that we've had last night and you're sober, things will be better between us."

"Just listen to me for a minute. Is it really fair to ask for my love and then just toss me out in the cold if you meet some man and decide that he's the one you really want? I can satisfy your needs now, but until you come to terms with who you really are, we can't be together that way. I can enjoy you now, but my love for you goes too deeply to know that there's a chance I could lose you forever. If you can't envision us having a lasting future together, then the sexual part of our relationship has to end, too."

"Why? Let's just live for today and not worry about tomorrow. Nothing is for certain in this life. Isn't that what you've always said? Take pleasure while you can?"

"I'm sober now, Sam, and I'm seeing things differently. My eyes are wide open and my needs and values have changed. I want to spend my life with only one person—you—and you can't promise me forever."

Samantha swallowed the lump rising in her throat. "I feel like I'm being split down the middle. I really need you, J.C."

J.C. folded her in her arms. "My love will always be here. Go find what you are searching for, and if you find out it's not what you wanted, then come back to my bed. I can't share your heart with a stranger any longer."

"What about last night, J.C.? Do you realize the depths of your passion? You were so intense. It had a whole new meaning. We've never made love like that before."

455-DRON

"I told you that I'm sober now. Everything is different . . . more intensified. And I also told you before we started that it was the last time. I'll just have to live with my memories."

"You've never said no to me before."

"Do you know how hard this is for me, Sam?" She gently brushed her lips over Samantha's, battling the impulses building within her. "I want all of you, not just a piece of you. Please understand."

Samantha pressed her mouth against J.C.'s, but J.C. abruptly broke away. "I'm going to get some sleep now. I'll use the spare room."

J.C. tossed and turned, fighting the urge to go to Samantha. Her mind finally drifted back to the night she first invited Samantha home with her. It was the first time she ever laid eyes on her. She'd been at Harve's, sipping at her drink and trying to work up enough courage to go over and talk to her. Usually she wasn't shy, but there was something about this woman that unnerved her. After forty-five minutes, when she was certain that Samantha wasn't waiting for someone, she casually sauntered over to her table. The scene played through her mind as though it had happened only yesterday.

"Hi, I'm J.C. I haven't seen you in here before."

"Hi," Samantha answered in a preoccupied tone of voice.

"Can I buy you a drink?" she offered.

"Yes, I guess so. Thanks." She looked into J.C.'s eyes and smiled.

The smile went straight to J.C.'s heart.

"I'm sorry, please sit down." She gestured to the empty chair, which J.C. was leaning over. "I'm usually not this rude, it's just that I've had a rough day."

"I know how that goes," J.C. answered. "So, do you have a name?"

"I'm sorry. Samantha."

"Glad to meet you, Samantha." She sat down, finding it hard to remove her gaze from this beautiful woman's face. She had class, and her type wasn't usually seen at Harve's. It wasn't that Harve's wasn't a nice bar; it just lacked an upscale social standing. And women who looked like Samantha generally didn't inhabit this section of the city. She was definitely out of her element here. "So, what brings you here?"

Samantha shrugged. "You don't want to hear my story." She picked up her wine glass and sipped at her drink, her eyes focused on J.C. J.C. felt herself becoming lost in them.

"I'd love to hear your story. You look like you could use a friend."

She sighed. "I need something."

"Maybe I can take care of that," J.C. said in a low voice.

"Excuse me?"

J.C. felt her face growing warm, and at the same time wanted to kick herself for making such an obvious pickup line. This woman was classy and needed to be treated as such. "Nothing. I only meant that I'm a good listener."

"Have you ever had your entire world come crashing down on you all at once?"

"I've been there. It can't be that bad."

Samantha lowered her eyes. "It can be," she whispered in a voice choked with emotion.

J.C. became uneasy. What had she gotten herself into? Maybe she should just finish her drink and walk away, but something deep within told her that she had to get to know this woman. It was much more than just a physical attraction.

A tear slid from Samantha's eye. Impulsively, J.C. grabbed her hand.

"Hey, you want to get out of here and go to my place where we can talk in private?"

She noticed Samantha's hesitation and held her hands up.

"I'm harmless. Promise."

"I suppose it would be all right."

J.C. pulled a few crumpled bills from her pocket and threw them on the table. "I don't live far from here, so we can walk."

455-DRON

She felt peculiar walking through the dark, dirty streets of her neighborhood with Samantha at her side. She tried to make idle conversation, but after a few minutes decided to relax and just savor this magnificent woman's presence. A few people called out greetings to her, and J.C. gave Samantha brief character descriptions. "I want to warn you that my apartment isn't much, but at least it's a place to lay my head."

"I'm sure it's fine," Samantha answered.

J.C. stopped in front of a run-down tenement. She dug into her pocket and pulled out her key, unlocked the door, then led Samantha through the stench-filled corridor until she reached her apartment. Once inside, she turned on a couple of lamps, then motioned to the sofa. "Can I get you something to drink?"

"No, thank you," Samantha replied as her eyes traveled around the cramped, disorderly room.

J.C. instantly wished she wouldn't have brought Samantha here to this dump. She should have sprung for a motel room, but that wouldn't have been proper for someone as elegant as Samantha. Maybe they should have just stayed at Harve's, and in all likelihood Samantha may have invited her to her home, which J.C. imagined to be like something out of a magazine. "So, Samantha, what brought you to Harve's?"

"I was riding around in a taxi all night, and I saw the sign for Harve's. It looked like a nice place, so I decided to stop in. I just wanted to forget my problems for a while. Haven't you ever done something like that?"

J.C. nodded. "I promised you that I'm a good listener, so if you want to talk about your problems, I'd like to help in any way I can," she offered.

Samantha shuddered. "Tonight is so hard for me. If I can get through this night I know I'll be okay."

"What's wrong?" J.C. asked softly.

"This entire year has been a nightmare. It's as though I'm only dreaming and seeing someone else's life, not mine. But then I look around and know that it really is my life, and I can't change what's happened."

"What happened?"

"You have enough problems of your own without taking on mine, too."

"I'm not going anywhere." She gave her a friendly smile. "Besides, sometimes it helps to share your burdens with someone else. You can get a better perspective on things."

She was thoughtful for a moment. "It's so hard. The three most important people in my life were all taken from me this year."

J.C. looked at her quizzically. "What, kids? You lost custody or something like that?"

"No, I don't have children."

J.C. stared blankly at her.

"My parents were killed in a plane crash overseas, and my fiancée was killed four months ago in a car accident in Canada. This is the first anniversary of my parents' deaths."

"I'm sorry," J.C. whispered. "Do you have any other family?"

"No." She looked at J.C., eyes brimming with tears. "I just needed a friend tonight."

"You must have loads of friends."

"Acquaintances, but not real friends." She grimaced. "Not the kind who are sincere and to whom you can confide your deepest thoughts."

"I'll be your friend."

"Thank you."

J.C. sat down next to her, her heart thudding hopefully in her chest. "I'll be whatever you want me to be," she whispered seductively.

"I don't understand." Samantha's eyes narrowed.

"Let me show you." J.C. put an arm around her, drawing her close as she savored the smell of her. She softly brushed her lips over Samantha's swanlike neck.

455-DRON

"What are you doing?" Samantha asked sharply, pushing her away.

J.C. was confused. "I'm sorry . . . I—I thought this is what you wanted when you agreed to come home with me."

Samantha's eyes widened. "What? Oh my God! Are you a lesbian? Did you think . . ." Her voice trailed off.

J.C.'s face reddened. "Look, I'm sorry. I thought you wanted to spend the night with me." She let her breath out in a rush. "What the hell were you doing in a gay bar if you didn't want to be hit on? Especially with your looks."

Samantha stood up. "I'd better be going."

J.C. swallowed hard. "Look, I'm sorry. If you want a friend, I'll be your friend. You don't have to go. I won't touch you. I'm perfectly harmless."

Samantha slowly shook her head. "I honestly didn't know I was in a gay bar. How could I be so naive?"

"Does it bother you that I'm gay? I mean, are you prejudiced?"

"I never really thought about it either way, but I'm certainly not prejudiced. It's a lifestyle I know nothing about."

"Why don't you let me fix you a drink and we can talk."

Samantha sat back down. "I'd like that." She smiled. "You're very likable, J.C."

"I don't think too many people will agree with you, but thanks anyway."

"So, tell me about yourself."

"There's nothing much to tell." She handed Samantha a glass of wine. "It's not as good as you're probably used to drinking, but I try to keep a bottle on hand for special guests."

"Thank you," Samantha said with a smile. "Now tell me who J.C. really is."

J.C. laughed. "I'm not sure you really want to know."

"Try me," Samantha answered as she settled back into the worn sofa.

"Well, I've been nowhere most of my life. Harve, the owner of Harve's Bar, has been like a father to me ever since I was a small child. He helps me out from time to time and is the only person who has always been there for me." She took a sip of her wine. "Let's see, I come from a large family. I haven't seen any of them for years and don't care if I ever do," she said bitterly.

"That's sad. Is it because you're gay?"

"No. I doubt they even know."

She looked hard at J.C.

"What?"

"How old are you?"

"Twenty-two," J.C. answered.

"This is probably going to sound ignorant, but when did you know you were gay?"

J.C. laughed at her question. "I guess I always knew but didn't understand. I found myself becoming physically attracted to women when I was about twelve. I had my first true love when I was fourteen. It lasted until she went to college. After a failed relationship, my first love and I tried to recapture what we'd had so many years before, but it didn't work out. We broke up six months ago. I guess we were just two lonely souls trying to regain what was familiar to us." She searched Samantha's face. "Do you know what I mean?"

"No, not really. There was no way you and your lover could make it work?"

She shook her head. "No, we grew up and drifted apart. Don't get me wrong, I'll always love her, but not in a sexual way. It's like she's a part of me."

"It sounds very passionate." She sipped at her wine. "When your friend went off to college, did you ever explore whether you had any feelings for men?"

"I thought my attraction and even sexual experience with my girlfriend was normal and something every girl would experience, and that it would pass." She grinned. "I actually believed it was one of those topics that were never spoken about. I dated boys, thinking that would put me on the track I assumed I was supposed to be on, but it didn't. So I finally accepted the fact that I was different from my girlfriends." She laughed again. "I felt sorry for them because they didn't know what they were missing."

Samantha gave her a warm smile.

"I learned to play the right games so no one would suspect the truth about me. Every time a boyfriend would suggest double dating, I found myself fantasizing all night about his friend's girlfriend and wishing I were the one with her. Then when I was about eighteen and my girlfriend went to college, I got involved with an older woman." She glanced at Samantha. "Is this upsetting you?"

"No," she gently answered. "It's just so sad. Is life hard?"

"It's not easy. But straight or gay, people still have to live their lives and still have problems."

"You don't have anyone in your life now? I mean, a girlfriend?"

She shook her head. "If I did I wouldn't have invited you here."

"What happened to the older woman?"

"It ended and we went our separate ways."

"That's when you got back with your high school love?"

She nodded.

"Do you ever get lonely, J.C.? Do you ever wish there was someone there for you whom you knew really cared about you and you could depend upon?"

"My middle name is loneliness."

"Do you go to church?"

J.C. smiled. "You certainly go from one topic to another."

Samantha laughed. "There's something about you—so open and honest—that makes me feel as though I've known you my whole life. I really would like us to be friends."

"I'd like that, too."

"So, what about church?"

"I used to go, but when I came out, I was shunned. So much for the golden rule of love one another. Murderers are more readily acceptable than I am," she answered caustically.

"I know. I quit going because all they seemed to want was my money, but didn't care about what I was going through."

"I'm sorry about your parents and boyfriend."

"Thanks."

J.C. felt herself becoming intensely attracted to this forbidden love. She ached to hold her and feel her creamy white flesh against her own. She struggled with her emotions but couldn't fight the feelings swelling within her chest. She carefully picked up Samantha's hand and held it in her own, wondering what sensations were running through Samantha right now.

Samantha gave her hand a gentle squeeze. J.C. interpreted it to mean that Samantha was feeling what she was feeling.

"You have the most beautiful eyes I have ever seen," she whispered.

"Thank you."

J.C. leaned forward and impetuously brushed her lips against Samantha's. When Samantha made no effort to stop her, she pressed her mouth tighter against hers.

Samantha jumped to her feet. "I thought you weren't going to try anything, that we were only going to be friends!"

J.C. was bewildered. "When you didn't stop me right away, I thought . . ."

"I need to get out of here." She grabbed her purse. "I'll get a cab."

Before J.C. had a chance to register what had just taken place, Samantha was gone. She walked around her tiny apartment in a stupor. She could still smell the perfume lingering in the air. She picked up the wine glass from which Samantha had drunk, seeing a faint smudge of lipstick where her mouth had been. Her face was etched into J.C.'s memory now, and her heart rejoiced with the recollection of her musical laugh.

J.C. spent the next week in an emotional torment she didn't understand. She couldn't get this woman out of her system. She knew she was being silly; she didn't even know her, but just the same, Samantha had a profound effect upon her. She kept herself holed up in her apartment, not even venturing out to Harve's. She doubted she would ever see her again, and it

455-DRON

filled her with a sadness she had never before known or would ever begin to understand.

Then one dreary, rainy night a knock came to her door. No one ever visited her, except a rare salesman, so she hesitantly opened the door. To her delight and shock Samantha stood on the other side. J.C. stared in disbelief.

"Well, are you going to let a friend in?" Samantha asked in a gentle voice.

J.C. was mystified. "I never thought I'd see you again."

"I was worried about you. I went to Harve's every night this week looking for you. No one had seen you."

"Why were you looking for me?" Her eyes searched Samantha's.

"Can I come in? It's damp out here."

"I'm sorry, certainly, come right in."

Samantha removed her raincoat. She wore a tight-fitting pair of jeans and a flannel shirt. "Do I look like I fit in now?"

J.C. grinned. "What's this all about?"

"I'm not even sure myself. I've been trying to figure it out all week. I'm being honest with you, J.C." She looked intently at her. "Are we still friends?"

"Always."

"Ever since you kissed me that night, I felt different. Something changed inside of me. That's why I didn't push you away at first. But I was terrified to act on those feelings. I never felt myself attracted to another woman before. I thought maybe it was because I was in a depressed state of mind, but then I started thinking about you constantly and wondering if you were thinking about me. My mind began to imagine things that maybe it shouldn't have been imagining."

"Can you put this into plain English for me?" J.C. asked with a grin.

"I don't know who or what I am anymore and I don't even care. The one thing I do know for certain is that I'm feeling a deep attraction for you. I don't conclude I'm gay. I'm not sure what I am. The only thing I know is that I had to see you."

J.C. sat down on the sofa and motioned her to sit beside her. She took Samantha's hands in her own. "Tell me what you want," she whispered, staring hopefully into those beautiful eyes.

Samantha swallowed hard. "I want to know your love, J.C., but I'm frightened."

J.C. brushed a loose strand of hair from Samantha's cheek, then softly kissed her as her hands slowly caressed the warm flesh she so desperately craved to touch. "Don't be afraid. I'll show you what love should be."

J.C. sat up and grabbed her cigarettes. After that night she and Samantha became a couple, but only in secret. They had been friends and lovers for five years and were almost inseparable, but now it had come to an end. The only thing that mattered was that Samantha had to determine what she really wanted. And J.C. would have to live with that choice.

455-DRON

CHAPTER FOUR

Ted slowly dialed the number, and after five rings the receiver was picked up.

"Hello," a breathless voice answered.

"Hello, this is Ted Jamison. I'm representing Joyce Markin. I understand that you're a friend of hers."

"You've got to be kidding! For all I care that bitch can rot in hell!"

He grimaced at the hostile voice. "Could I meet with you some time tomorrow afternoon, Mrs. Sebastion?" he asked, ignoring her remark.

Darcy paused for a moment. "I suppose, but believe me, if you're looking for an ally, you're asking the wrong person."

"I just need some background information."

She laughed. "I can give you plenty, but I doubt it will be the kind of information you're seeking."

"What time would be good for you?"

"Anytime after five."

Ted glanced at his appointment book. "That will be fine. I'll see you in my office tomorrow."

"I'd prefer if you could come to my home."

He frowned. "All right. I have your address, so I'll see you tomorrow afternoon."

He hung up the phone, poured a stiff drink, then settled his muscular frame on his leather sofa. He pulled on his chin as he pondered the short but strange conversation with Darcy Sebastion. He hoped that Darcy was the only enemy J.C. had. He was counting on her friends and acquaintances to help in her defense.

He finished his drink, then dialed Samantha Wheeler's apartment.

"Hello," a sleepy voice answered.

"This is Ted Jamison. I'm sorry to disturb you at such a late hour, Samantha."

"That's quite all right. What can I do for you, Mr. Jamison?"

"Please call me Ted. Is J.C. still awake?" he asked.

"No, she's sleeping. Why? Is something wrong?"

"No. I just needed some information."

"Is there anything I can help you with?"

"Maybe. I'm meeting with Darcy Sebastion tomorrow afternoon. I was hoping that she would help in J.C.'s defense, but she's very bitter where J.C. is concerned. I wasn't aware of any conflict between those two. J.C. has never mentioned any animosity between Darcy and herself. Can you fill me in?"

Samantha sighed. "Darcy has been giving J.C. a hard time. This has been going on for months . . . long before J.C. was indicted. They just don't care for one another. It's as simple as that. Darcy doesn't like anyone below her social class."

Ted was thoughtful for a moment. "Let me see if I have this straight. Darcy only tolerates J.C. because of your friendship with J.C.?"

"That's about the size of it. Darcy's one of those people who always has to be right about everything. She sees J.C. as not being good enough for me because she wasn't born into money and social standing the way she and I were. It's actually quite sad, because deep down J.C. is a good person. She's had a hard life and has some rough edges, but she can be very sensitive."

"How about J.C.'s other friends?" he questioned. "Do you think they'll cooperate?"

"J.C. is a loner. She has more acquaintances than friends. I'm not sure if there is anyone who will come forward to help her."

"Well, at least she has you. Is it all right if I stop over tomorrow morning to speak with J.C.? I'll be bringing some people with me from Alcoholics Anonymous who would like to meet her and make arrangements to transport her to some meetings. She needs to keep attending her meetings."

"Certainly."

"I'll see you about ten, then."

Samantha hung up the phone, turned out the lights, and walked slowly toward the master bedroom. She paused outside of the guest bedroom, using all of her willpower not to enter the room and J.C.'s bed. She needed J.C. like she had never needed anyone before. She desperately tried to see J.C.'s point of view. J.C. needed and certainly deserved so much more than she could offer her right now. Her inability to make a choice wasn't fair to either of them. J.C. wanted security. She couldn't give her forever, but she could give her one night at a time. For the past five years they had shared so much together, but she always warned J.C. that a commitment was something she couldn't offer her. Samantha had to deal with her own sexual identity and define who she really was, and very soon. There was no way she could continue to live like this. It was too painful. The more she suffered, J.C. suffered ten times more acutely; it was an agony that Samantha found almost unbearable. She wouldn't intentionally hurt J.C. for the world, but she knew that she was, and still a part of her refused to let her go. She had to make a choice and soon, for both of their sakes.

* * *

"J.C., I'd like you to meet Mark Evans and Christy Fellows. They've agreed to help you settle into some AA meetings."

"Have you ever been to any meetings, J.C.?" Christy asked.

"In jail." J.C. cautiously observed the woman, wondering if her statement shocked her. But the look on Christy's face showed that it hadn't even fazed her.

"They run a very good program for the inmates. I've gone to several myself," she answered.

"How long have you been sober, J.C.?" Mark asked.

"Not long."

"Why don't we pick you up about seven and take you to a meeting tonight," Christy said with a bright smile.

She nodded. "Okay, I'll be ready."

"Would you two like some coffee?" Samantha offered.

Mark glanced at his watch. "No, thanks, we've got another appointment." He patted J.C.'s shoulder. "Hang in there and we'll see you tonight. Here's Christy's and my phone numbers. Call anytime day or night."

"Thank you," J.C. answered in a quiet voice.

After they left, J.C. turned to Ted. "They seem like nice people."

"They are," he assured her. "If I didn't trust them completely, I never would have brought them here."

"Would you like some coffee, Ted?" Samantha asked.

"Yes, I would, and then I have a few things we need to discuss, J.C."

"Sure."

"We need to talk about your past and any friends you can think of who might give good character references."

J.C. laughed. "I'll surely rot in prison, then."

Samantha set a tray on the table. "Fresh pot."

"Good," Ted said with a smile as he took the cup she offered him. "You must have someone close to you who really knows you, J.C."

She lowered her eyes. "I did have, but he's dead. The only other person who truly knows me is Samantha."

"There's no one else?"

"Just a friend I haven't seen in years. I don't even know where she's living anymore."

Ted turned his attention to Samantha, his gaze traveling to the low cut sheer blouse she wore. "I need to get to know the both of you better. I strive to have a good relationship with my clients. If I don't, then it's difficult to defend someone when I don't even know anything about that person."

"Have you ever had to defend someone you personally didn't care for?" Samantha curiously asked.

455-DRON

"More times than I care to admit. If an attorney and client don't have total honesty between them, it can be disastrous in court. It's one of those surprises every attorney dreads. That's why I need to have your full cooperation, J.C.," he said, turning his attention back to her.

"What more do you want from me, blood?" she retorted. "I never socialized much."

Ted set his coffee cup down. "I need some straight answers, J.C. Enough games! If you think I'm being tough on you, then wait until you take the stand!"

She looked imploringly at Samantha. "What kinds of questions will they ask me? They won't ask me questions about my sex life . . . will they?"

"J.C., please tell Ted everything. You promised to cooperate. He can't help you if you don't tell him everything," she pleaded.

"I'm not certain what you'll be asked. I can, and will, object to questions pertaining to your intimate relationships, but that doesn't mean it won't come out. If I know everything up front, it'll be easier on both of us."

She shook her head. "I don't understand what any of this has to do with my being charged with murder."

He let his breath out slowly. "I know that it doesn't make much sense, but believe me, I've seen juries convict, or free, someone just on something that was blurted out in testimony even though the judge had ruled it inadmissible. Of course, they aren't supposed to, but they're only human. The jury will be paying close attention to everything you say and what others are saying about you. How you compose yourself is extremely important."

"I understand, but I think our justice system sucks—no offense."

"I have to agree with you that many times I've been frustrated with a decision, but it all comes down to those twelve people. But let me assure you, the jury selection process will be fair. These people won't know you from Eve so what ever is said, they will be evaluating on your reactions as well."

"So if I'm convicted it's because they think I killed Harve."

"It's not as simple as that. They have to know it beyond any doubt." He folded his hands. "I need you to answer some questions now, honestly and to the best of your recollection."

"I don't have any other choice."

"No, J.C., you don't. So, are you ready?"

She took a sip from her cup, then set it back down. "Go ahead. Ask away."

Samantha winked at her.

"Tell me about your sex life."

J.C. felt her face flush. "It's normal."

"Nothing unusual?"

She shrugged her shoulders. "I don't follow you."

"Have all of your sexual relationships been with men?"

"No. Some were with women," she answered, staring into her coffee cup. "No, that's a lie," she quickly added, "only women. I'm a lesbian."

"Why do you sleep with women?"

She laughed. "That's absurd!" She blinked hard. "For the same reason you do."

Ted wondered if she was about to cry.

"This has nothing to do with the case," she grumbled.

"I need to know the real you, J.C.," he said softly.

She stood up. "Look, I'm not some kind of pervert! Why can't people understand that? I'm still a fucking human being with feelings! I just prefer sex with a woman instead of a man!" She blinked again. "Do you think I chose to be what I am? My life has been hell because of it!" Her voice quieted. "Do you think I've enjoyed living most of my life in secret? Do you have any conception of how that feels? When I finally meet the woman I want to spend the rest of my life with, she tells me we have to keep our love affair a secret."

"Is this other woman a lesbian?" he asked.

"She doesn't know what the hell she is and that makes it even harder."

Ted frowned. "I agree it must be difficult for you, J.C."

455-DRON

"I would love to walk down the street hand in hand with my lover, to sit in the park with my arm around her, or to kiss her in the moonlight. But all of those things are denied."

He eyed her closely as she spoke. "Have you ever had an affair with Darcy Sebastion?"

"Give me a break!" she grimaced. "She's about as straight and narrow-minded as they come." She inhaled deeply. "Even if she was gay, she isn't my type."

"Explain that to me."

"Come on, you're not an ignorant man."

"No, I'm not, but I don't understand the lifestyle." He leaned back in his chair. "Educate me. Now's your chance."

She looked suspiciously at him. "You must know some gay people."

He remained silent, staring at her.

"I am not attracted to every gay woman I meet. She still has to have certain qualities that make me want to be with her. You don't want every woman you meet, do you?"

"No, I don't." He was thoughtful for a moment. "Why don't you and Darcy Sebastion get along?"

J.C. ran her hand through her hair, pushing it straight back from her forehead as she eyed him. "We had a misunderstanding about someone. I thought she had a thing going on with someone I was very close to."

Ted kept her steady gaze. "I thought you said Darcy was straight."

"She is, but I was jealous."

"Can you fill me in?" he prompted.

"Sam," J.C. pleaded as she broke her gaze with Ted.

"Go ahead. It's all right," Samantha coaxed.

J.C.'s voice trembled as she clasped her perspiring palms together. "I thought that Darcy was having an affair with Samantha." Her voice broke. "I went crazy, I guess. I saw them sitting together in a way that I totally blew out of proportion. Samantha and I had been arguing and we weren't seeing each other anymore at the time, and I couldn't stand the pain of knowing she could be giving her love to someone else. I didn't understand why they were doing this to me." Her eyes pleaded with his. "I told you that you would never understand."

"I'm trying to, J.C.," he answered softly.

She swallowed hard. "I don't know why I did it. Without even thinking, I walked over to Samantha and didn't even give her a chance to speak. I caused her to injure herself." A tear rolled down her cheek. "I was filled with a rage I had never felt before. Jealousy was consuming me. I wanted to hold her and just be close to her, but all I could think about was getting out of there. I pushed her out of my way and didn't know she'd gotten hurt. I was out of control and I couldn't stop myself!" She covered her face with her hands.

Ted watched closely as Samantha walked over to J.C. and knelt down beside her. "J.C.," he began slowly, carefully formulating his question as tactfully as he could. "Are you and Samantha now involved in a sexual relationship?"

She dabbed at her eyes with a tissue. "No, it's over between us. We're just friends now." She kept her eyes down. She couldn't bear to look at Samantha.

"When did you two meet?" he asked.

"We've known one another for a few years," Samantha answered.

"Then . . . well, I should ask you this, Samantha," he said slowly. "Have you ever been involved sexually with Darcy Sebastion?"

"No, of course not," she stated.

"I'm confused." He frowned.

"J.C. is the only woman I've ever been sexually involved with. I'd better start at the beginning," she replied. "J.C. and I met under very unusual circumstances. I was going through a difficult time and went out one night, not really caring where I ended up. I decided to stop for a drink and, inadvertently, ended up in a gay bar—Harve's. I met J.C. that night and we've been friends ever since."

"Had you been with a woman before your affair with J.C.?"

"No. J.C. is the only woman I have ever slept with."

J.C. sat upright. "I don't see what any of this has to do with my trial."

"The prosecutor, Stuart Brewster, may try to use some of this information against you, J.C.." He looked at Samantha. "Is there anything else I should know?"

"Eventually I asked J.C. to move in with me." She stopped abruptly. "Do you need details about our sex life?"

"No, Samantha," he answered softly.

"I wish I could explain the way it really was. Too many people refuse to even try to understand this kind of love. They depict it as deviate and perverse, but it's not that way at all. I was closer to J.C. than I had ever been to anyone in my entire life. She saw me through my pain and never bolted, even when I hit severe bouts of depression."

"Why did your relationship end?"

She sighed and took a sip of her coffee, then carefully set the cup down. "I had doubts about who I really was and what I really wanted. I still had strong feelings towards men and, during this time, other problems were beginning to surface, but I feel it's only fair to let J.C. explain."

Ted focused once again on J.C. "What happened?" he asked.

J.C. looked into Ted's eyes and thought she could see some concern there for her, but she wasn't certain. Maybe it was for Samantha. She'd been watching the way he looked at Samantha and felt the sexual tension between them. She cleared her throat. "My drinking bothered Sam, and she was constantly on my back about it." She cleared her throat again, then took a deep breath. "She asked me to move out. Weeks before, I noticed how she and Darcy seemed to be getting closer, and they were spending a lot of time together. I felt shut out. I felt like Samantha had totally rejected me, and I was so lonely." She glanced at Samantha as she relived her anguish. "I was insane with jealousy; no matter where I went, I would see them together and it ate me up inside."

Her voice quivered. "I would give her up to a man if I had to, but not another woman."

"But if she had chosen another woman over you, J.C., you would have had to accept it. It happens everyday in relationships, whether heterosexual or homosexual," Ted answered.

"I know, but she was such a part of me—I'd never felt so connected to another human being like I was to her." She pushed her hair from her brow. "I can't explain it. I was tortured . . . I couldn't go on."

"What happened?"

"The night before Harve's murder, I decided to go to a different bar. It was out of my class, but I thought, what the hell, Sam had taken me there before. When I walked in, I saw her and Darcy sitting together at a table for two, in the corner. I tried to control my emotions, to pretend that it didn't matter." She looked at Samantha again. "But it did matter. I—I walked over to their table and that's when I grabbed Sam. I wanted her to want only me."

"Were you badly injured, Samantha?"

"No," she replied.

J.C. quickly stood up, spilling her cup of coffee. "Look, Ted, I don't see what any of this has to do with my fucking trial!"

"J.C.! He's only trying to help you. He can't unless he knows the facts."

J.C. shot Samantha a dirty look as she tucked her flannel shirt into her faded jeans. Thunder roared in the distance; the darkening clouds matched her dismal mood. "Are you blind, for God's sake? He couldn't care less about me. I've been sitting here all morning watching him. It's you he's interested in hearing about! Open your eyes!"

Samantha smoothed her skirt over her knees as she stole a glance at Ted. Ted's face reddened as he adjusted his tie. They both looked uncomfortable, only confirming her suspicions.

Ted cleared his throat. "I don't need to know every detail, but it's better for me if I have an accurate account of your behavior in the days leading up to Harvey Barthow's death." He lit a cigarette, then turned to J.C. "If you think that I don't care about you, then you're terribly mistaken. I need to know about your past in order to represent you appropriately. I don't want to see you ripped to shreds on the stand for something I wasn't aware of."

J.C. saw the dark circles under his eyes. His face was drawn as he watched her, which now made her feel uncomfortable.

"J.C., I won't lie to you. Your case is difficult. I do believe you when you say you were framed, but I need to know an exact account of your whereabouts the night of Harvey Barthow's murder. Up to this point you've avoided answering the question. Please tell me everything that happened that night."

She stared out of the window, watching the rain pound against it. "I stopped in Harve's for a couple of drinks that night. I saw Samantha. I needed to talk to her."

"Did you?" he asked.

She nodded. "It wasn't a friendly conversation and I was upset when I left the bar. I walked to my apartment. I remember that it was raining and cold. I passed out shortly after I got home. Anyway, when I woke up, I needed a drink and I couldn't find anything in my apartment, so I came over here to ask Sam for a drink. She gave me one, then we got into an argument and she kicked me out. The next thing that I remember is waking up in jail." She walked back over to the chair and sat down. "I don't know what happened after I left here." Her jaw grew firm. "And that's the absolute truth."

Ted was pensive as he looked at her, then back to Samantha. "Not recalling your actions for several hours is not going to help you, J.C. You were arrested outside of Harvey Barthow's apartment. Also, not knowing what happened during those hours should give you a clue as to the drastic effect alcohol is having on your life."

"I'm not drinking now," she said. "You know that."

"Make certain that you don't. Stick with Mark and Christy; they'll help you." He stood up. "I've got an early afternoon appointment." He turned to Samantha and smiled warmly at her. "Thank you for the coffee."

"You're very welcome, Ted." She returned his smile.

Samantha walked him to the door, and J.C. caught the way they looked at one another. She knew deep in her heart that Samantha had found her man; a man who would give her what she craved, a man who could give her the kind of love J.C. was incapable of giving her.

* * *

Ted was thoughtful on his drive to Darcy Sebastion's, his mind retracing the morning's conversation with J.C. and Samantha. He wondered if he would ever be able to understand what those two women had shared. More importantly, he wondered if he would ever understand how Samantha could want the love of a woman and a man at the same time. He was as attracted to women as J.C. was and could relate more to her feelings than to Samantha's. Both women were attractive and could easily snap up just about any man they set their sights on. He shook his head. J.C. had a sharper edge than Samantha, but that was partly because of their diverse upbringings. If the situation had been reversed, he was positive that Samantha would still be gentle and kind and J.C. would be more polished, but still with a roughness about her. Not that she wasn't an intelligent woman; she just wasn't willing to let anyone see anything deeper than what was on the outside.

He recalled how caring Samantha had been to J.C. when J.C. spoke of her mistreatment of Samantha. J.C. had become so pale; he knew, without doubt, that she regretted what she had done. Samantha had immediately been at her side, holding her head to her bosom as she stroked J.C.'s hair. He could almost understand J.C.'s jealousy, and if Samantha had been his woman, he would've felt the same way. But his reaction would have been handled differently. He wouldn't have hurt her for the world.

55-DRON

Feelings were stirring deep within himself, feelings he tried to ignore but couldn't. Samantha Wheeler was grabbing hold of his heart and he couldn't let that happen. It wasn't ethical. He had to put aside his own desires and concentrate only on J.C.

He rubbed his eyes as he mentally prepared himself for his meeting with Darcy. He didn't know what to expect after his brief conversation with her the previous night. He rechecked the address in his appointment book, then pulled into the driveway.

Ted rang the doorbell as he observed the architecture of the old house. The grounds were beautifully landscaped and included a tennis court and golf course. Darcy Sebastion was wealthy, but not as wealthy as her home established her to be. He couldn't understand why a woman of her social standing would inhabit seedy little bars late at night. He understood how Samantha had ended up at Harve's, but not Darcy Sebastion. Something didn't mix. He could feel it. He was overcome with an odd feeling that somehow this woman was an important link in J.C.'s case, but he would have to be on his guard with her.

Darcy cautiously opened the door. "May I help you?"

"Yes, I'm Ted Jamison. We have an appointment."

"Of course, Mr. Jamison, please come in." She smiled brightly as she ushered him into her spacious living room. The marble topped coffee table held a pitcher of martinis and two empty glasses. "Do make yourself comfortable," she offered. She poured two drinks, then handed one to him and seated herself on the sofa across from him. "Please let me know if you'd like anything. I've given my housekeeper the night off, but I'm certain I could prepare a snack."

"No, I'm fine, thank you." He was aware that she wanted to make certain that he was conscious of her presence as she sat sipping at her drink, gazing at him. She curled her feet beneath herself, exposing much of her chubby thigh in the process. She didn't bother to adjust the scarlet negligee she wore under a light wrap.

He tried to pull his gaze away from her. Her face was beautiful, but in a different way from Samantha's. Darcy was dark complexioned and her hazel eyes sparkled merrily. Her beauty was a rich, spoiled beauty and she looked like the snobbish image of wealth. Her arresting looks might have been almost perfect if it weren't for the extra fifteen pounds she carried. "I came to ask you a few questions about J.C. Markin," he stated.

"What would you like to know?" she asked.

"Why don't you two get along?" He set the untouched drink on the table.

"It's obvious, isn't it? She comes from the wrong side of the tracks. She's a joke." She fluffed a pillow, then placed it behind her back. "I do feel sorry for her, though."

Her remarks annoyed him. He thought again about Samantha. She didn't care where a person came from and seemed to offer her help to anyone in need, but obviously Darcy wouldn't. Darcy preferred to flaunt her wealth on those less fortunate, making them envious of her. "Why do you go to bars such as Harve's? Isn't that out of your social class?" he asked.

"Why not?" she laughed. "Samantha and I have always been close friends, and one day she happened to introduce her new friend to me. Samantha had been going through a series of tragic losses and ended up in this quaint little bar one night where she met J.C. All J.C. talked about was Harve's, and Samantha began going there regularly with her and seemed infatuated with the place. I thought she would snap out of it, but when she didn't I decided to see for myself what charm Harve's had that fascinated Samantha. At the time I didn't realize that it was J.C. who held her fascination. I found Harve's to be very unique. After an evening there I could return home and be grateful for what I had, knowing that I didn't have to return to some stinking, cockroach-infested hole in the wall like J.C. did."

Ted felt anger rising within him but quickly suppressed it. He had to admire the woman for her honesty, as egotistical as it was. "It is my understanding that you and J.C. got along when you two first met. What happened?"

"Whomever told you that must be dreaming. We never got along. I only tolerated her for Samantha's sake. I tried in vain to

55-DRON

get Samantha to end her ridiculous relationship with J.C. She had her fling on the wild side, and now it was time for her to get back to her own world," she answered bitterly.

"Why would her friendship with J.C. affect her life negatively?" he asked.

"You do know that J.C. likes women, don't you?" she asked surprised. "Not only that, but she has absolutely nothing to offer anyone except for her body."

"Yes, I do know that she's a lesbian, but that is beside the point."

"J.C. will only drag Samantha down to her level. Samantha should've never involved herself with her. As far as I'm concerned, J.C. needs to be locked away for the rest of her life. I don't know why Samantha didn't have her arrested when she hurt her. I witnessed the incident. I was willing to testify on Samantha's behalf, but once again she felt sorry for J.C. and refused to stand up for herself." She shook her head. "I don't know what you expect me to say in J.C.'s defense, Mr. Jamison. I don't have one humane word for that woman. I will be happy to testify, but not for her. She is insanely jealous of Samantha and has some sick notion that Samantha and I are having an affair."

Ted frowned. "I conclude that we have nothing further to discuss, Mrs. Sebastion, but I would like to thank you for your time." He stood up, eyeing her closely. "One more question. Do you think J.C. and Samantha are still lovers?" He watched her dark eyes flash momentarily.

"I certainly hope not." She patted the space next to her. "You don't have to leave so soon, do you? I thought that it would be nice if we got to know one another a little bit better," she said seductively. "Maybe you can convince me of J.C.'s redeeming qualities."

"I have to leave," he answered.

"You might like what you see," she countered as she began undoing the straps of her gown.

"I don't think so."

"What's the matter? Are you afraid?" She ran the tip of her tongue invitingly over her full lips.

"No, Mrs. Sebastion, I'm not afraid. I'm just not interested."

"I may be persuaded to testify in J.C.'s behalf."

He laughed. "Is that a bribe? Because if it is, I don't take kindly to bribes."

"Your client doesn't stand a chance!"

"I'll be the judge of that." He walked to the door and turned, but she had not followed him. He opened the door, stepped outside and stood in front of the house for a few seconds, thinking about his bizarre meeting. Darcy Sebastion was a peculiar woman, but there was more to her than met the eye. He had to dig deeper. He got into his car and stared at the house as he backed down the driveway.

* * *

J.C. nervously looked around the room. The smiling community reaching for her hand, welcoming her, were all strangers to her, or maybe it was the other way around. They were so exuberant it made her feel like an intruder. Could she even hope that maybe someday she would be able to share their happiness? Christy and Mark introduced her to so many people she lost count. She pasted a smile on her face as she took the hands extended to her. She was relieved when it was time to be seated. As everyone stated their names and admitted their dependency on alcohol, she awaited her turn. She stood up and felt all eyes turn to her. "Hi, my name is J.C. and I'm an alcoholic."

"Thank you for coming tonight, J.C.," the meeting leader said. "Is this your first meeting?"

"No, I've been to meetings before."

"Good, just hang in there one day at a time, and thank you for coming tonight. Would you like to share your story with us? Or do you have a topic we can discuss?"

"Yes, I'd like to share my story," she said nervously. She avoided eye contact as the words spilled from her lips. Talking to these strangers seemed natural and right. She lost track of time as she relived her life for them, letting them know the pains and horrors she had suffered. When she finished, she felt clean and relieved. A burden had been lifted from her and she knew that she truly belonged. Renewed hope surged through her. No matter what happened to her now, or in the future, she wouldn't be alone.

After the meeting, she mingled with several other women. She was sipping a cup of coffee when she felt a hand on her shoulder. She turned to greet the stranger.

"Glad to see you here, J.C."

She looked, stunned, at the familiar face, then quickly set the cup on a table. "Jo!" She threw her arms around the woman's neck. "I didn't see you!"

Jo grinned. "I was sitting in the back. I got here late, but not too late to hear your story." She patted her back. "I'm sorry about Harve."

"Thanks."

"If it's any consolation, I know you had nothing to do with his death."

"Thanks, Jo, I've just got to convince the rest of the world," she answered.

"Well, you're on the right track with AA." She smiled and grabbed J.C.'s hand. "Let's get out of here and go to a diner so we can catch up. How long has it been? Over five years?"

"I have to let Mark and Christy know. They drove me here."

"Okay. Go find them and I'll get my jacket."

* * *

Ted hung up the telephone, then leaned back in his chair. He was beginning to worry that J.C. didn't stand a chance. She would need a miracle, or someone aside from Samantha Wheeler, who was willing to give an exemplary character reference. He had talked to everyone who had even had a fleeting acquaintance with her, but none could give him what he needed; what she needed. Those who did care for her didn't want to become involved. Most feared, because of what they would be asked, they would cause her more harm than good. He prayed she would stay out of trouble and continue her AA meetings. Maybe he could use that in her defense, show that she truly was changing her way of life, but still he needed to find a way for her to remember those missing hours.

His thoughts drifted to Samantha. He couldn't get her out of his mind, and even if it wasn't ethical he still desired to know her better not professionally, but personally. He didn't understand her past sexual relationship with J.C., but he accepted it. He had no other choice. He pondered asking her out, feeling like a schoolboy pacing the floor, afraid to pick up the telephone. He lit a cigarette and pondered how he would ask her to see him on a personal level. If she said no, then he would get her out of his system, but if he didn't make the call, then he would never know how she might feel about him. He finished his cigarette and picked up the phone, slowly punching in her number as his palms moistened.

"Hello."

"Hi, Samantha. This is Ted."

"Is everything all right?" she asked anxiously.

"Everything is fine."

"Do you have any news about J.C.'s trial?"

"Not yet," he replied.

"J.C. isn't back from her meeting. I can have her call you when she returns."

"I didn't call to speak to J.C., Samantha."

"Do you need more information about her? I've already told—"

"No," he interrupted. "I'm calling personally, not professionally," he explained. "I'd like to take you to dinner tomorrow night if you're free." He held his breath as he awaited her reply.

"I'd love to," she said softly.

"Good. Is seven o'clock all right for you?"

"Seven will be perfect."

55-DRON

"I'll see you tomorrow night, then."

"Goodnight, Ted."

He was grinning as he hung up the telephone.

* * *

"How long have you been going to AA?" J.C. asked, stirring cream into her coffee.

"Almost a year now," Jo answered.

"No wonder I haven't seen you around for awhile," J.C. laughed.

"As though you missed me," she teased. "It's been more like five years."

"I did miss you. You were the only person I could talk to, except for Samantha."

Jo swallowed a bite of hamburger, and then wiped her mouth. She placed the napkin on the table. "Did you ever tell Samantha about us?"

She shook her head. "It was so long ago, and as I recall, a very unstable relationship between us at the end."

"We had a lot of good times together, though."

"Yes, Jo, we did. And we managed to stay friends for all these years."

"Why didn't you ever get in touch with me after you and Samantha got together? We've always been friends. I was hurt that you shut me out of your life."

"I'm sorry, Jo. Samantha was so different. I was trying to be something I wasn't and in the process left my past, including you, behind. I've always regretted my decision. Ever since the first day we met, you've been the only stability in my life."

"Sometimes I wish we could have worked it out together."

J.C. saw the pained look in her friend's eyes. "I don't think we could have made it. We're too much alike, but we had our fourteen-year-old passion . . . our raging hormones."

Jo shrugged. "At least I have my memories." She took another bite of her burger. "And you popping in and out of my life." She swallowed. "This time, woman, I refuse to let you disappear for years at a time. You don't know how worried I've been about you since your arrest. I wanted to be there for you, but I didn't want to interfere because of Samantha."

"I wish you could have been there for me. I went through a horrible detox." She shuddered at the memory.

Jo patted her hand affectionately but said nothing.

"Are you with anyone now?" J.C. finally asked.

"No, I broke it off with Barb after I joined AA. It was very destructive. Barb was very abusive and it seemed when I quit drinking, she began drinking more. If I stayed with her I'd be jeopardizing my own sobriety. She didn't like me sober, but I think it only took some of the fun of drinking away from her."

"I'm sorry."

"Don't be. I'm sort of dating someone now. I'm taking it very slowly, though. Rachel knows what I went through for two years with Barb and she's very patient with me, and so understanding. She hasn't pushed for a commitment and even though I've given her the option to date others, I know that deep down she wants a commitment."

"Doesn't that bother you to think she may decide to see someone else?"

"Yeah, but so far she hasn't seen anyone else. So far, so good," she laughed. "But the thought is always in the back of my mind that she might meet someone else, and I'll lose her completely."

"Then why don't you just give her a commitment if you know she's the right one?" J.C. reasoned. "Come on, Jo, what's the problem? She sounds perfect."

She slowly shook her head. "I honestly don't know. I care deeply for her, but I'm still not certain if I can make that kind of commitment to anyone. Pledging myself to only one person for the rest of my life scares the hell out of me."

"If she's the right one, you'll want to do anything to keep her. Picture how you'll feel if someday she tells you she's found someone else."

55-DRON

She smiled. "Must be you and Samantha have that ideal bond, huh?"

"I can only wish," she answered sullenly. "We did for five years, but I blew it."

"I'm sorry." She touched J.C.'s hand. "Do you want to talk about it?"

She shrugged. "There's nothing much to say. My drinking caused problems between us. I was the one who wanted a commitment, but Samantha couldn't give me one."

"Why?" Jo asked incredulously. "You were together for five years!"

J.C.'s tone became hostile. "She doesn't know whether she wants a man or a woman!"

"That's absurd!" Jo exclaimed. "She's with you for five years, but doesn't know if she wants you or a man? Now I've heard everything!" She shook her head incredulously. "That must have crushed you."

"It doesn't make living there easy."

"Why don't you move out?"

"I would, but I can't. It's a condition of my bail release."

"Oh, God! That's got to be unbearable."

"At least I can go to meetings and see people. That helps."

"We can go together whenever you want to. I can take you to some other ones I go to where the people are just as great as they are at Southside."

"I'd like that," J.C. grinned.

"Mind if I smoke?" Jo asked.

"No, but I'll mind if you don't offer me one." J.C. took the cigarette Jo lit for her as she examined her ex-lover closely. Jo's beauty seemed to flourish with age. Her auburn hair hung loosely over her shoulders and her milky-white skin was flawless. "You're beautiful," J.C. whispered.

"What?"

J.C.'s face grew warm. "I'm sorry—I," she stuttered.

Jo laughed. "I know that was a compliment, and I thank you for it. It just took me by surprise."

She cleared her throat. "I was thinking out loud, but it's the truth. Age only makes you more beautiful."

Jo blushed. "Thank you, J.C. When we were together I often wondered if you even knew what I looked like."

"Yes, looking through alcohol enhanced eyes can really distort one's true vision."

Jo chuckled. "Do you remember that chick . . . what was her name? Oh, yeah, Donna. You brought her home one night to sleep on the couch. I hadn't gone out that night because we were having our usual argument."

"Oh no! Don't remind me!" J.C. pleaded.

Jo's face grew crimson with laughter. "You came to bed and tried to make me jealous by saying if I didn't want you, you would sleep in the living room because you knew Donna would want you."

"Unfortunately, I remember," she grinned.

"I said, 'Go then, if that's the kind of relationship you want.' You got out of bed and went to the living room. A few minutes later you come tearing back into the bedroom accusing me of doing something to change Donna's appearance." She choked with laughter. "I'll never forget what you said, not in a million years. You looked me in the eye and as serious as anyone could be said, 'Jo, that is the ugliest chick I've ever seen! What did you do to her? What did you put in her drink to make her so damned homely?' It took me hours to explain to you that she was the same woman you had picked up and brought home to sleep on the couch."

J.C. laughed uncontrollably. "We sure as hell had some bizarre times together."

"Yeah, then we grew up," she said, smiling.

"We grew older, but definitely not wiser."

"Hey, who needs wisdom? We had so much fun together." She looked at her watch. "I'd better get you home. Do you want to go to a meeting tomorrow night? I can pick you up."

"I'd like that, Jo."

55-DRON

"Great!" She grabbed her car keys from the table, then turned to J.C. "Can I ask you something?" she said nervously.

"You know you can ask me anything, Jo."

"After we broke up, did you ever miss me? Did you ever think about me?"

J.C. looked into her beautiful sea green eyes. "More than you'll ever know."

* * *

J.C. yawned as she poured a cup of coffee.

"Tired?"

She turned. "Hi, Sam. Yeah, I ran into an old friend and we went for coffee after the meeting."

"Mark and Christy didn't bring you home?"

"I'm a big girl, Sam."

"Do I know the friend you ran into?"

"No, she was before you."

"Why didn't you call? I was worried."

J.C. eyed her doubtfully. "Is it actually concern for my well-being, Samantha, or are you jealous because I was with another woman?"

"I'm not jealous, J.C. You have every right to see your friends."

"Even if it's someone who used to be more than just a friend?"

"It's your business." She poured a cup of coffee. "How was the meeting?"

J.C. saw the fleeting look of hurt cross her eyes. "Good."

"Ted called last night."

"Now what?" she asked irritably.

"It wasn't about the case." She looked at J.C.

"What, then?"

"He asked me out."

"On a date? Did you accept?"

"Yes, I did."

"I guess you've found your man," she whispered. She picked up her cup and walked out of the kitchen. She would never let Samantha see the vulnerable side of her again, nor would she let her know how it affected her to think of Samantha severing everything they had shared together. It was over—final—and J.C. had to find a way to live with the pain. Only this time it would be much more difficult. She was sober. Her old standby—whiskey—wasn't around to rescue her from the lonely nights anymore or sooth the cold ache in her heart. Now she had to stand up and face this torture on her own, with her emotions twisted and crying out in agony. She had to fight this battle on her own, a battle she wasn't looking forward to, knowing her only weapon was her sobriety. She had to keep her defenses up and not let Samantha know the grief that was swallowing her.

55-DRON

CHAPTER FIVE

"Good morning, J.C.," Samantha said brightly. "Jenny's coming over to clean this morning."

"Do you want me to leave?"

"Don't be ridiculous. I thought you got along with Jenny."

"I do. She's nice."

"Then why would you think you had to leave?"

She shrugged her shoulders. "I don't know. It was a stupid thing to say, I suppose."

"Do you want some breakfast?"

"I'm not hungry."

"So, tell me about the meeting."

"What's to tell? A bunch of people who used to get drunk sit around trying not to drink, but sometimes thinking about it." She avoided Samantha's penetrating gaze. "We help each other not to pick up a drink."

"You're not thinking about it, are you?'

She smirked. "I don't think the day will ever come when I don't think about it. But if you mean am I going to drink, then the answer is no, not today. One day at a time is the motto."

"What's wrong with you, J.C.? Ever since I told you I was going out with Ted tonight, you've been acting strangely."

She eyed Samantha closely. "What do you want from me? I don't care who you see. There's nothing between us. You had your fun with me, now you can run to your man."

Samantha grabbed her arm. "J.C., is that what you really think? That I was playing games? What we shared is very special to me. I'm sorry you don't believe me, but I never used you. I have always been honest with you. I told you I didn't know what I wanted, but I will never regret what we had together."

J.C. pulled her arm free. "As soon as I save enough money—that is, if I'm found innocent—I'll move."

"You don't have to, J.C. I enjoy being with you."

She stared wide-eyed at her. "You're playing head games with me."

"I am not. What about you? You won't even tell me about your ex-girlfriend. Why haven't you mentioned her to me before?"

"She wasn't important." She lowered her eyes. "With you it was as though everything was fresh and new. I put that phase of my life behind me."

"Can I ask you one question?"

J.C. looked into her eyes.

"How long after you broke up with . . ."

"Jo."

"How long after did you start seeing me?"

"About six months."

"There was no one else?"

"No, I never cheated."

"How many in the six month period between Jo and me?"

"What difference does it make?"

"It doesn't. I just want to know."

"I don't know. I had a lot of one-night stands that didn't mean anything. That was it."

Samantha lowered her eyes. "I'm sorry if I've hurt you, J.C. That was never my intention."

"Hey, don't worry about it." She walked over to Samantha and placed a hand on her shoulder, then with her other hand raised Samantha's chin until she was gazing into her eyes. "I love you enough to let you go." She shrugged. "Besides, I've always been a survivor and always will be."

* * *

Samantha laughed at Ted's anecdotes. "And I thought lawyers didn't have a sense of humor."

"In this business sometimes a sense of humor is the only thing that can keep you from losing your mind. You can't even begin to imagine some of the characters who walk through my door every morning."

"So, tell me, what did you think when you saw J.C.'s file?"

He rolled his eyes. "Honestly?"

She nodded.

"My first reaction was 'Why me, God?' But there's something about her, after you break down the self-imposed barrier, that's innocent. My gut reaction was to dig deeper. And I'm still digging. There's a very important piece of the puzzle missing, but I don't intend to give up until I find it."

"She can act so tough, but that's all it is, just an act."

"All we can do at this point is wait for the break we need."

Samantha leaned closer to him. "What do you really think her chances are, Ted?"

He frowned. "I can't even call it at this point. A miracle would help."

"That's not very encouraging."

"I wish I could tell you that everything is going in her favor, but it's not."

Samantha picked up her coffee cup and slowly brought it to her lips. Ted watched her, wanting to ease her mind, but he couldn't lie to her. She had to know the truth.

"Is J.C. attending meetings regularly?"

"Yes."

"Mark and Christy are terrific people. They'll help her."

"She hasn't been going with them. She ran into an old friend and has been going with her."

He raised his eyebrows. "Maybe her friend can help by giving a character reference."

"I never thought of that."

"I'll call J.C. tomorrow to see about arranging a meeting with her friend." He motioned for the waiter. "We'd better get going if we want to get to the theater on time."

* * *

J.C. watched Jo maneuver easily through the large group, giving everyone she saw a bright smile and cheery hello. She smiled to herself. That was just like Jo. Always the helper and the caregiver—giving, but hardly ever taking. She wondered if she and Jo would still be together if she hadn't been a drinker back then. But then, Jo too had been a heavy drinker. They were both adolescents when they first met, and maybe the drinking was the only thing that had kept them together, though it had also driven them apart.

J.C. had to keep her emotions in check; especially now. She was heading into dangerous territory. She couldn't get romantically involved with Jo again; it wouldn't be fair to either of them. Her feelings for Samantha were still raw, and she couldn't use her best friend to satisfy the longing within, because that was all it would be. She truly loved Jo, but it was a different love than what she felt for Samantha. Just the same, though, she could sense the passion rising within her. But was it truly passion, or just the need to feel the warm soft flesh of a woman next to her skin again, especially the woman who had opened her up to this special love so many years before?

"Hey, wake up," Jo laughed, tapping her shoulder. "The meeting's starting." She thrust a steaming cup of coffee into J.C.'s hands.

J.C. grinned. "Just daydreaming. Thanks for the coffee."

"I remember how you like it," she said with a wink.

For the next hour they absorbed the speaker's life story, then afterwards stood around sipping more coffee and munching cookies.

"Want to get out of here?" Jo whispered close to her ear. "How about a movie?"

"That would be a welcome relief. I love everybody here, but I need a change of pace. My only social life revolves around AA."

"Let's go." She slipped an arm around J.C. and led her towards the door.

"J.C., can I talk to you for a minute?" Christy touched her arm.

"Sure, Christy," she answered.

"Do you have a sponsor yet?"

She shook her head. "I don't really know too many people well enough yet."

"Well, think about getting one, okay?"

J.C. nodded. "Can you be my sponsor? I feel comfortable with you and you already know everything there is to know about me."

"I'd love to, but if you ever change your mind and find someone you'd rather have, don't be afraid to tell me." She smiled brightly. "I'll call you tomorrow."

"I won't find anyone I'd rather have," J.C. promised.

"Thank you. Are you leaving all ready?"

"Yeah, we're going to catch a movie."

"Good," Christy answered. "Stick with Jo, J.C. She's a good person and I'm a personal friend of her sponsor."

"Guess I'd better watch it or you'll be reporting me to Gloria," Jo said with a laugh.

"You two have fun," Christy said, then turned to say goodbye to a skinny young man.

"She's nice," J.C. said as they walked to the car.

"She really is. She's had a horrible life, but she's pulled herself together." She grabbed J.C.'s hand. "You'll make it, too."

"Thank you, Jo. Having you for a friend is the only good thing that's ever happened to me."

* * *

Ted opened the door to Samantha's apartment. "Can I see you again?" he asked.

"I'd like that. Would you like to come in for a drink?" she offered.

"I would, but I've got an early morning appointment. I'll take a rain check though."

"You've got it."

He bent down and softly brushed his lips against hers. "Goodnight."

"Goodnight, Ted." She shut the door, then walked into her bedroom and slipped out of her clothes. She threw a bathrobe on and strolled into the kitchen to make a cup of tea.

J.C. sauntered into the kitchen. "I didn't think you'd be home yet."

"I got here a little while ago. Where were you? The meeting ended three hours ago. I thought you were in bed."

J.C. ignored the worried tone in Samantha's voice. "Jo and I went to a movie, then we got a bite to eat."

Samantha eyed her closely. "You and Jo seem to be spending a lot of time together."

"Are you jealous?" she asked pointedly.

Samantha blinked hard. "No." She poured steaming water into a cup. "Do you want some tea?"

"No, you should know by now that I hate tea."

"That's right. I'm sorry."

"No need to apologize. So, did you and Ted have a good time?"

"It was nice," she answered distractedly.

J.C. stared at her for a few seconds. "Is something wrong?"

"No, of course not." She turned to J.C., flashing a bright smile. "Ted's a very nice man. He's fun to be with."

"Good."

"He's going to call you tomorrow. He wants to know if Jo would give a character reference for you."

Her eyes narrowed. "What good would it do?"

"She obviously knows what a decent person you are or she wouldn't be spending so much time with you. Besides, you and she go back a long way."

"I suppose."

"How was the meeting?"

"You ask me the same question every night. The meeting was good as it always is."

"Did you see Christy and Mark?"

"Yes, they were there. Christy said she'd be my sponsor."

"That's wonderful! I'm happy to see all the support you're getting, J.C. I know you're worried about the trial, but it's going to work out. You'll see."

J.C. ran her hand through her hair and yawned. "I hope so. I think I'll go to bed. See you in the morning."

"Goodnight, J.C." Samatha watched her leave as a sadness she didn't understand filtered through her heart.

The next afternoon Samantha tiredly rubbed her throbbing temples as she settled herself onto the sofa. "Did you get in touch with Jo?" she asked, keeping her voice light.

"Yes, she's coming over after work. Ted said he'd talk to her here. That's all right with you, isn't it?"

"Of course," she answered with a forced smile. "It'll also give me a chance to meet her."

J.C. eyed her suspiciously. "Samantha, what's wrong with you? You haven't been acting like yourself for days now." She frowned. "Have I done something to piss you off?"

"Everything's fine," she assured her.

"Jo and I are just friends, if that's what you're worried about." She peered at her, noticing how quickly Samantha tried to avert her eyes.

"I wasn't even thinking about that. Besides, it's none of my business."

J.C. saw the haunted look in Samantha's eyes even though she tried to hide it. "Are you sure?"

She nodded. "You have a right to see whomever you want to, just as I do."

She watched as Samantha rose to her feet and left the room. Something was bothering her, but Samantha didn't seem to want to confide in her. She remembered when she and Samantha had shared everything. There had been no secrets between them. If something bothered one of them, the other was always there to offer comfort and support. Now those times seemed so long ago, almost like it was in a different time span and a different life. Time marched on, and they had severed the deep ties that bound them together in what J.C. had hoped would be for all of eternity. She followed her into the kitchen.

"Do you want me to fix something?" Samantha offered.

"Just coffee will be fine," J.C. said, then hurried to the door when the bell sounded. "Hi, Jo. Thanks for coming."

Samantha walked back into the living room and listened to their muffled voices in the foyer. She tried to calm the queasiness in her stomach, at the same time wondering why she felt so hopelessly depressed. She was thankful that J.C. had Jo, but if the truth were known, the pangs of jealousy were rising within her.

"Samantha, I'd like you to meet Jo." J.C.'s arm was draped loosely across Jo's back as they walked into the room.

Samantha was surprised with Jo's appearance. She wasn't quite sure what she had expected, but this certainly wasn't it. Jo was impeccably dressed in a business suit, the skirt at the proper length, and her makeup was as perfect as the rest of her matching accessories. Her eyes sparkled. She was beautiful. "It's nice to finally meet you, Jo."

"It's nice to meet you, Samantha." Jo gently shook her hand. "I've heard so much about you."

"Please have a seat." She watched J.C. lead her to the sofa. Jo seated herself in a ladylike manner while J.C. plopped boyishly next to her. J.C. seemed so comfortable and relaxed next to Jo. "Would you like some coffee while we wait for Ted?"

"Yes, please." Jo smiled. "You have a lovely apartment, Samantha."

"Thank you. I'll get the coffee."

"I'll help," J.C. said, jumping to her feet.

In the kitchen, Samantha was silent as she placed cups on a tray.

"Is something wrong, Sam?" J.C. asked in a soft voice.

She shook her head. "She's very nice, J.C., and beautiful."

"I know."

"Why did you . . . never mind."

"Why did I what?" J.C. questioned.

"Nothing. It's none of my business."

J.C. grabbed her arm. "What, Samantha?" she whispered. "What were you going to say?"

The doorbell sounded, giving Samantha an excuse not to answer her. "That must be Ted." She hurried to the door.

J.C. set the rest of the items on the tray, and then carried it into the living room.

"How's it going, J.C.?" Ted asked.

She smiled. "Very well." She turned in Jo's direction. "This is Jo O'Brien—Jo, Ted Jamison."

"Nice to meet you, Jo," he said warmly. "I assume J.C. informed you why I asked to meet with you."

"Yes, she did. I want to help her in any way possible," she replied, giving J.C.'s hand a squeeze.

J.C. didn't remove her hand. Samantha's own hand shook slightly as she poured the coffee. She hoped no one noticed, then realized they weren't even looking in her direction. She handed J.C. a cup, and her skin tingled when J.C.'s hand brushed against hers. If J.C. sensed it, she didn't let on. Her attention was focused on Jo.

Samantha sat in a chair and for the next forty-five minutes listened to Jo's raving reviews of J.C. Ted laughed at one of Jo's recollections. "You're going to be a big help in J.C.'s defense, Jo. I appreciate everything you've told me."

She smiled. "I only regret not being around much for the past few years, but it wasn't easy for me when we ended our relationship, even though we knew we'd always be friends."

J.C. grabbed her hand. "But we managed to remain even better friends now."

Jo smiled at her. "And that's something that can never be destroyed."

"In any event, Jo," Ted said, "I know that you're a positive influence on J.C."

"Thank you."

Ted closed his notebook, then placed it into his briefcase. "I'll be in touch, Jo, and thanks again for your help."

"Any time." She stood up. "I'd better be going if I'm going to make the meeting tonight." She looked at J.C. "Do you want to get some dinner before we go? I can go change and pick you up in forty-five minutes."

"Sounds great," she answered. "I'll walk you out."

Ted noticed Samantha's somber mood. "Are you all right?" His voice was soft.

She smiled. "Yes. Jo seems like a very nice person."

"She certainly isn't what I had pictured. Where did she say she works? The North Side Bank?"

"Yes."

"She's classier than I had imagined."

Samantha was thoughtful for a moment. "They must have had a very special relationship to have remained so close."

"Didn't J.C. ever mention her to you?"

She shook her head. "No. The first time I even heard her name was when she gave J.C. a ride home one night from a meeting."

"Hmm, maybe their breakup was difficult for J.C. and she put it behind her."

"I suppose, but I'm just pleased that she has someone to talk to."

"Yes, I haven't seen her this happy in months." He looked at his watch. "Would you like to have some dinner with me?"

She smiled. "Why don't I fix us something here?"

"Sounds good to me. Want me to help? I'm a whiz in the kitchen. We bachelors can fend pretty well for ourselves, you know."

She laughed. "Come on," she said, grabbing his arm and leading him towards the kitchen.

* * *

J.C. hummed softly as she watched Jo maneuver the car into a tight parking space.

"Told you I could do it, Markin," she teased.

"Just luck," J.C. laughed. She stepped out of the car and waited for Jo. "Want to come up for awhile?"

"No, I'd better not—early day tomorrow." She walked with J.C. to the lobby. "Go after her, J.C."

J.C. stopped in her tracks. "What?"

"Samantha. She obviously cares about you. I could sense it tonight. Don't let her go."

"You're way off base on that one, Jo. She's made it perfectly clear that she doesn't want a relationship. Besides, she's dating Ted."

"I don't think she knows what she truly wants, and if she makes a choice I'll bet it's you she chooses."

"And I should stay in the background and pine away for her until she decides? No, I can't do that any longer. I need to go on with my life."

She was silent as they stepped into the lobby. "J.C., I've got to tell you something."

"What?"

She searched her eyes. "I still have feelings for you. You were my first, remember?"

"You were my first, too, Jo. We were fourteen years old." She threw her head back. "My, God, do you realize how long we've been together off and on throughout the years?"

"Why didn't you try to call me even once when you were with Samantha?"

Her eyes clouded. "I didn't want to hurt you, Jo. I know this is going to sound stupid, but I've never been as close to anyone as I have been to you. It's as though we are a part of each other and always will be. That's why we still could remain friends even when the sexual part of our relationship ended. I felt bad that you hadn't found your special someone like I had, and I didn't want to rub your nose in my happiness."

"J.C., we agreed a long time ago that we want what's best for one another, and if we couldn't make it together, we would still remain together in spirit; if not lovers, then always friends. And as your best friend and soulmate, I would have loved to share in your happiness whether I had found someone or not."

"I know. I'm sorry." She gave her shoulder a squeeze, then impulsively leaned over and tenderly kissed her.

Jo looked into her eyes but said nothing as J.C. led her to a deserted, shadowy corner. She placed her hands on either side of Jo's face, then kissed her deeply.

Jo threw her arms around her neck. "I wish this was forever, J.C., but I know it can't be."

J.C. instantly backed away from her. "I shouldn't have done that. I'm sorry."

Jo placed a finger to J.C.'s lips. "Don't ever be sorry, J.C. No one will ever take our memories. And I know we'll never be fourteen again, but sometimes I wish we could go back to that time when life was simpler."

"We don't know what's going to happen, but I know that I do need and want you in my life, Jo, and I never want us to be separated again."

"No matter what happens . . . soulmates, just like we said years ago."

J.C. slipped into the apartment and silently stole down the hallway to her bedroom. She climbed into bed but couldn't sleep. Her thoughts took her to her past—the past from which she had tried to escape, but the same past that had brought Jo into her life. Jo was a lifeline to her back then. She smiled with the memory.

Jo had walked up to her one day in school, asking to borrow a pencil. J.C. hadn't noticed her before, but back then she didn't notice much of anything. She gave her the pencil, and Jo struck up a conversation. J.C. soon found out how much Jo liked talking. Jo had just recently moved to the city but didn't care for the kids in

55-DRON

school. J.C. had noticed how Jo carried herself; she wasn't like the other girls, and there was a natural freshness about her. J.C. immediately took a liking to her, and soon they became fast friends. Every day after school they walked side by side to the Westwood Diner. After sliding into a booth they ordered cokes and watched the jocks and cheerleaders come in thinking they owned the world. Jo made up funny rhymes about them, making J.C. fill in the blanks. J.C. always worried that she couldn't hold up her end of the conversation, but Jo's natural ability to keep it going eased her mind. One day, though, Jo's usual bantering didn't come.

"Do you ever feel like you're someone else?" Jo had asked.

J.C. laughed. "I don't even feel like me most of the time, so I don't know what that would feel like."

"I feel different from the other girls in school. Do you know what I mean?"

J.C. nodded. "Yeah."

"I don't like all the things that my parents think I should be liking—like boys."

"I don't like boys either."

"Do you ever think there's something wrong with you?"

J.C. shrugged her shoulders. "I never thought about it much one way or the other."

"What do you think about?" Jo asked softly.

"I don't know. Probably just getting out of my house as soon as I can."

"Don't you get along with your family?"

"Sometimes."

Jo sipped at her cola. J.C. watched her closely, wondering what she was really thinking. "Do you get along with your family?"

"Yeah, they're okay."

"Is something wrong?"

"Nah." Jo shook her head. "I was just thinking. I'll tell you about it this weekend."

"Why not now?"

"It's not the right time or place."

J.C. had walked her to the bus stop, knowing that Jo was heading to an upscale part of the city while she was left to wander through the dim, dirty streets to her own home. It was what people referred to as the bad side of town, or the other side of the tracks.

The following weekend they spent hours together at the diner laughing, talking, and listening to music as usual. J.C. thoroughly enjoyed her new friend's company, and Jo positively influenced her outlook on life. "Do you think you could spend the night sometime?" J.C. asked.

"That would be fun. Sure. My parents won't care. I can do just about anything I want to do."

"Great. When do you want to stay?"

"How about tonight?" Jo asked.

J.C. smiled. "Come on. You can call your parents from my house."

"Don't you have to ask permission for me to stay?"

"No. No one pays much attention to what I do."

Later she led Jo up the narrow stairs to her bedroom. Once inside she sprawled across the bed. "Want to listen to some music?" She didn't wait for a reply and turned on the radio.

Jo lay on the bed next to her. "This is a nice room."

"I decorated it myself," she laughed. "Can't you tell?"

Jo looked at a few posters, then turned her attention back to J.C. "Do you ever wonder about things that you shouldn't wonder about?"

She propped her face in her hands. "That's what gets me into so much trouble." She grinned.

"What do you think about?" Jo asked, sprawling out so that they were facing one another.

"A lot of things."

Jo propped her chin on her hands as she gazed into J.C.'s eyes. "Tell me the worst thing you've ever wondered about."

She shrugged. "I don't know."

"Come on," she prodded. "Tell me what you would never tell anyone else. Unless you don't trust me."

"I trust you."

"Then tell me and I'll tell you."

She took a deep breath. "Okay, but you'll think I'm weird."

"I promise I won't . . . no matter what you tell me."

J.C. picked at the bedspread. "Sometimes I wonder how it would be to . . ." Her face flushed.

"What?"

She looked down at the bedspread. "To . . . to kiss a woman. I told you you'd think I'm weird," she quickly added.

Jo laughed. "I've thought about that for a long time."

"You have?" J.C. stared at her wide-eyed.

She nodded. "Remember Miss Coleson? She was our English substitute last term?"

"Yeah, I remember her."

"I had this thing for her . . . like a crush. It was hell going to school every day, but it was also the bright spot of my day."

"I had fantasies about her, too."

"You did?"

"Yeah." J.C.'s face reddened.

"Have you ever felt that way about a guy?"

She shook her head. "No, I told you I was weird."

"I haven't either."

"Really?"

"Really, so if you're weird than I must be, too."

J.C. smiled, suddenly feeling better about herself.

"Have you ever, you know, kissed a girl?"

"No, have you?"

"No."

They were silent for a few minutes, listening to the music as J.C.'s heart thumped wildly in her chest. "Can I kiss you?" she finally whispered.

Jo touched her cheek. "I'd like that, J.C."

J.C. leaned toward her and gently brushed her lips against Jo's.

"That was nice, J.C." She shifted her position, moving next to her, then softly placed a hand on J.C.'s back. She gently stroked her back for a few minutes.

J.C.'s body rippled with feelings she didn't understand; feelings that had lain dormant but now needed to be released. She turned onto her back and pulled Jo down on top of her. She wrapped her arms around Jo's body as their lips met in a fervent kiss, a kiss that would forever stay engraved in J.C.'s memories.

J.C. grabbed her cigarettes and lit one. She slowly exhaled, remembering the youth and passion she had shared with Jo. That night they had both innocently given themselves to one another with no shame or regrets. And for the years that followed, they remained steadfast friends even when their lives and circumstances had led them to others. They agreed early on that they would never let their passion for one another interfere with their friendship. Even though it hadn't always been easy, they gave one another the wings needed to fly and explore. Neither made a lifetime commitment to one another. The only commitment made was to always remain friends.

But there were times when too much time had elapsed without them seeing one another. It had always hurt when they had gone their separate ways, but deep down they had always remained in one another's hearts. What they had shared was a special awakening to their own sexuality, and it was a moment in time that J.C. wouldn't have traded for anything. Jo had breathed life into her veins.

She put her cigarette out, then pulled the blanket up to her chin. When Samantha Wheeler entered her life, J.C. knew that she was ready to make a commitment. This was the woman she wanted to spend the rest of her life with. She yearned for her; her heart was tortured now. Jo could give her everything but the lifelong commitment she needed. She and Jo were too much alike to stay together as a couple.

She tossed and turned, finally falling into a fitful sleep.

55-DRON

CHAPTER SIX

Ted Jamison set down the file. He couldn't concentrate; his mind wandered to thoughts of Samantha. He was growing closer to her. He would never fully understand her past relationship with J.C., but he couldn't stop the feelings developing for her, either. There was something about her that made him fall in love with her, and he couldn't have stopped it even if he'd wanted to. There. He'd said it. He had fallen in love with her and it scared the hell out of him. She affected him like no other woman ever had. They had dated for weeks now, but their relationship had never developed beyond a simple goodnight kiss. Samantha constantly worried about J.C., and any conversation they had always ended up back to J.C.. He had to turn that tide.

He was pleased with J.C.'s progress. She was faithfully attending AA meetings and seemed to be developing a close relationship with Jo O'Brien, but he was still worried. Her case was complex. His thoughts wandered back to Samantha. He needed to hear her beautiful lilting voice. He picked up the telephone and dialed her number.

"Hi, Samantha . . . I'd like to see you."

"Is something wrong, Ted? Is it about J.C.'s trial?"

"No, nothing like that. I'd just like to see you . . . a date . . . no business." He sighed. "We always end up discussing J.C.'s impending trial. I'd like us to go out and talk about nothing but ourselves. Let's just relax and have a good time for a change."

"Why don't you come over and we can talk, Ted."

He smiled. "I'll be there in twenty minutes."

Samantha hung up the phone.

“Ted’s coming over again?” J.C. asked. “I was planning to go to a late meeting with Jo, then get together with my sponsor.”

“What does that have to do with me, J.C.?”

“I don’t know. I thought he wanted to talk about the trial.”

“He wants to talk to me, J.C. It’s not always about the trial, so you can go to your meeting.” She smiled.

“You two are becoming chummy,” she scowled.

“I like Ted very much,” she replied. “I enjoy his company.”

“Do you think he’s getting anywhere with my case, Sam?” She wrung her hands. “I’m scared. I could go to prison.”

“You won’t,” Samantha assured her. “”Ted is a good lawyer. Something will come out to prove your innocence. Have faith in him.”

“You’re right.” She walked over to the window and gazed at the traffic below. “Can I ask you something?”

“It depends.”

“Will you give me an honest answer?”

“I’ve never lied to you, J.C.”

J.C. turned and looked at her. “Have you and Ted slept together?” She stared into Samantha’s eyes.

Her eyebrows furrowed. “No. We’ve never even come close.”

“Do you care about him?”

“Of course I do. He’s a very warm, sensitive man. I’ve grown very fond of him.”

“If he asked you to, would you sleep with him?”

She blushed. “I don’t know. It would depend on the circumstances. Maybe. Why are you asking so many questions?”

She shrugged.

“I could ask you the same questions.”

“Meaning?”

“You and Jo.”

“We’ve always been friends,” J.C. said defensively.

“Yes, but you did have a relationship that goes way back.”

“We aren’t sleeping together.”

“But you’ve thought about it?” Samantha asked.

55-DRON

J.C. flushed. "I'm lonely."

"And Jo is available," Samantha said in an icy tone.

"Dammit, Sam, we haven't done anything. What do you want from me?"

She shook her head. "Nothing. You wouldn't tell me the truth even if I asked."

J.C. felt her anger rise. "And just what is it that you want to know?" she furiously asked.

"Why you never told me about her. It doesn't make sense."

"What's to know? She was my first. I was her first. We built a bond together."

"But you seem so happy and contented together."

"Yes, we have a solid friendship."

"Why did you two go your separate ways, then?"

"We'll always love each other, but we were both growing in different directions."

"Seems to me like you have an awful lot in common in this stage of your life."

She let her breath out. "Look, Sam, I'm not fucking Jo, but if I were, it wouldn't be any of your business."

"But if I were sleeping with Ted, it would be yours?"

"No, it wouldn't. But it's an entirely different situation."

"Why? Because Ted is a man?"

"Yes, because he is a man. For God's sake, Samantha, you have to make a choice. How fair have you been to me?"

"I think I've been very fair to you. I've never lied about my needs."

J.C. threw her hands up. "You can't have it both ways. Not anymore!"

"I never said I wanted it both ways."

J.C. walked over to Samantha and stood directly in front of her. "Then just tell me that you don't want me! I can't move forward with my own life until I'm absolutely certain that you don't want me."

Samantha lowered her eyes. "Then would you run back to Jo?"

"That's not fair!" J.C. sank into a chair, covering her face with her hands. "Damn you, Samantha Wheeler! Why are you doing this to me?"

Before Samantha could answer, the doorbell rang. "I'll bet that's Ted now," she said with a smile as she walked to the door.

J.C. sat on the sofa as the voices in the entrance hall came closer. Samantha acted so differently around Ted. She remembered in high school how the girls were always swooning over the boys. That was how Samantha was acting—like some sex-starved teenager. It bothered J.C. more than she cared to admit. She wondered if she should have considered keeping the sexual part of her and Samantha's relationship. But what good would that have done? Samantha would've still slept with Ted if that were her desire. She needed to have all of Samantha, not just a piece of her. And her yearnings to hold her again grew deeper everyday. A raging fire burned within her that only Samantha could put out. She could turn to Jo to satisfy the ache within her, but it would only be a temporary satisfaction, and what would it really prove? Only that she was weak. And it wouldn't be fair to Jo.

As they aged, she and Jo were finding more in common, but as much as she did love Jo it wasn't the love she had found with Samantha. And Jo was looking for a deeper love, too. She and Jo would only be together if their hearts weren't with another. That had always been their understanding. She was jealous of Ted, and she didn't know how to handle her emotions. This was new territory to her, and Samantha controlled the outcome of her life. She needed to know what Samantha's choice would be, and soon. Not knowing was eating her alive.

"Hello, J.C.," Ted said brightly. "Do you have plans for tonight?"

"AA," she answered with a weak smile as she watched how his gaze traveled over Samantha's voluptuous body. A body that she knew he wanted, desired, craved just as she did. But which of them would be the ultimate victor for Samantha's heart?

"The meetings seem to be helping you. Or is it your friend Jo?"

Her eyes narrowed. “I don’t know. Maybe both. At least I’m not drinking now, am I?” she asked sarcastically.

He patted her shoulder. “Don’t be so hard on yourself, J.C. I’m doing everything possible to prove your innocence. Once the trial is behind you, we’ll spend some time mapping out your future plans. You have so many options available to you.”

“I hope it works out.” She glanced at the clock. “I’ve got to get ready. Excuse me.”

Samantha watched as J.C. left the room. “Please make yourself comfortable, Ted. I’ve got to talk to her for a minute. She’s been in a strange mood all day.”

“Of course,” he answered.

Samantha walked into J.C.’s bedroom. “What’s wrong?” she asked.

J.C. turned. “Don’t you believe in knocking?”

“I’m sorry.” She noticed, as J.C. slid her slender legs into a pair of jeans, how thin she had become these past months. And she recalled how many times her own hands had traveled over those legs. Her pulse quickened, but she quickly composed herself. “Is something bothering you?”

J.C. shook her head emphatically. “I’m all right.”

“I know you well enough to know when something’s bothering you. You can’t hide your emotions from me,” she said gently. J.C. pulled a jersey over her head. Samantha yearned to cling to that strong back again as she always had after J.C.’s passionate lovemaking.

“I’m just trying to accept the fact that I’ve lost you.”

“J.C., you don’t know how many nights I’ve lain in my bed praying for you to come to me.”

J.C. faced her. “Why didn’t you come to me?”

“I practically got down on my hands and knees and begged you that last night. How do you think I felt when you refused me?”

“You know why I refused you. It was the hardest thing I ever had to do. But you can’t promise me forever. Your feelings for me aren’t the same as mine are for you.”

“I’ve been honest with you.”

She sighed tiredly. "You have to decide what you really want—a woman or a man."

"I'm trying. I just don't know anymore. I love you and everything we've shared, but Ted is very desirable."

"I won't wait forever."

Samantha looked intently at her. "I remember once when you said you would wait forever."

J.C. blinked. "It hurts too much, Sam."

* * *

"This is nice, Ted," Samantha said, enjoying the peaceful silence.

Ted put an arm around her shoulder and pulled her close. She relaxed against his firm chest. Her head, lying gently against his shoulder, filled him with a tender longing. He had been waiting for this moment since the day he first laid eyes on her. "I want you, Samantha," he whispered hoarsely, turning her head until her eyes met his. He gently kissed her. "You can't imagine how many times I've longed to hold you in my arms. I don't care about the past, only now. Only this very moment matters."

* * *

J.C. walked into the lobby disappointed that Christy had to cancel their get-together. She didn't want to be home this early, but she knew Jo was worn-out and needed to get some rest.

"Let's find a movie or something," Jo suggested.

J.C. smiled at her. "No. You've got to get up early, and lately I've been monopolizing all your time. No wonder Rachel is giving you a hard time," she teased.

Jo rolled her eyes. "Rachel doesn't know what she wants. I told her to let me know when she figures it out." She laughed.

"You know what she wants, Jo. The same thing I want from Samantha."

Jo groaned. "The big C."

J.C. nodded. "You know that's the reason you and I had a great sexual relationship. We knew that we never had to have a commitment because we were friends first and foremost, even if we found someone else. We could still keep our friendship. Do you remember the first time we made love?"

"I'll never forget it." Her eyes glistened. "It was as though I finally knew myself; who I really was."

"And do you remember our vow?"

"That even without the sex we would always be one no matter where our lives took us," Jo answered. "But our lovemaking was so intense. Maybe that's what I'm looking for, J.C. I'm trying to recapture what you and I had."

"It'll happen," J.C. assured her.

Jo took her arm. "We share everything together. What's the matter with us? Why couldn't you and I make it together in a lasting relationship?"

She shook her head. "We're both too independent. We have great sex and conversation, everything two people could possibly want, but we can't live together in a commitment." She was thoughtful for a moment. "Maybe it's fear."

"Fear?" Jo asked.

"Think about it for a minute. If it didn't work out, then we wouldn't have what we have together today."

"I'm not sure I understand, but somewhere I'm sure it makes sense."

"Let's just always cherish what we had. Go to Rachel. Make wild passionate love to her, Jo. If she's the right one, you'll know it."

"That's what scares me. How will I know for certain?"

"When you know that you can't stand the thought of being apart from her. When her needs and wants surpass your own."

"You're the best, J.C."

"Make sure you tell the jury that," she said with a wink. "Now get going, and I'll see you tomorrow night."

Jo hurried to her car. J.C. debated whether she should go up to the apartment or find something to do to kill some time.

Samantha didn't expect her home for at least another couple of hours. Her mind drifted to Samantha and Ted. She wasn't certain how she would react if she walked into the apartment and found them together. Her thoughts of them together, making love, were almost unbearable and made her edgy and uncomfortable. She fought back the hot tears, which threatened. Couldn't Samantha see the hurting loneliness that was consuming her soul? Samantha was willing to give her body to her, but that wasn't enough; she wanted her heart. She couldn't settle for just a piece of her.

The need for a drink permeated her consciousness. She was fighting a losing battle. Whenever the going got tough, she had always picked up a drink, but it had been months now. She was scared. She knew she should call someone for help, but she couldn't. Her agony wouldn't let her think rationally.

She walked out of the lobby and to the corner liquor store.

* * *

"I want to know everything about you, Samantha," Ted said softly. "You've never told me much about yourself."

"We've been so absorbed with J.C.," she answered. "And I wasn't certain how you truly felt about me because of my past with her."

He hugged her. "Samantha," he whispered, "nothing could ever change the way I feel about you. I thought that maybe you didn't care for me. I've got to be honest. I don't understand your past with J.C., but God knows you've had your share of pain in the past, too. I don't know if your loss of your parents and fiancée had anything to do with your turning to J.C. at that time, and it doesn't matter to me anymore."

She sighed wistfully. "It's difficult to explain, Ted. In the beginning, I was so confused that I would have done anything to be rid of the terrible pain I was suffering. I was empty and void of any feeling. I was numb and didn't know if I would ever feel any emotion again. For months I depended entirely upon J.C. She stood by me through all of my dark moods, and when

I was certain I was losing my mind she was still there. No matter what I did, she stood by me—comforting, nurturing me back to who I truly was. She was my healer. She never once asked me for anything, but freely gave all the love she had to give to me. All she wants is someone to love her with the same capacity she loves. She is very insecure, even though she will never admit it. Her life is so complicated that if I were she, I know I would have given up years ago. I'm not that strong. But her strength is what sustains her. I'll never be ashamed of what she and I shared. Don't ever expect me to be."

He listened to the loyalty in her voice as he gently caressed her arm. "I want you, Samantha."

She smiled shyly and sipped at her wine. He looked into her eyes and saw the flames from the fire they had lit earlier dancing in them. She touched his cheek, making him feel like a live current coursed through his body.

"I want you to know that I do care for you, Ted," she said. "When I'm with you I feel content and safe."

He smiled as he bent his head and met her waiting lips, desire filling him as his tongue found hers. His heart raced as he reached under her blouse and gently fondled her breasts. "I want to make love to you," he whispered.

"Yes," she said, aware that her body wasn't coming alive at his touch. She needed to get J.C. out of her mind but images of J.C.'s body were flooding her thoughts. She needed to concentrate on Ted. He was the one she was with, not J.C.

J.C. listened outside the apartment door, and when she heard no sounds coming from within assumed that Samantha and Ted had gone out after all. She unlocked the door, then quietly closed it behind herself. She walked into the living room and flicked on a light. The sight of Ted and Samantha startled her.

"Excuse me," she said hoarsely. She looked away from Ted's naked body, but her eyes stayed glued on Samantha's. She couldn't break her gaze. Her chest grew heavy as her heart slowly cracked, then broke.

Samantha turned her head away from J.C.'s penetrating eyes. She couldn't bear to look into that dark, hurting gaze. She felt humiliated and ashamed, like she had just been caught cheating on her lover. Maybe she had. She felt sick inside. This was the answer she had been seeking. She was aroused with Ted's attraction to her, but the minute he had touched her she could only think of J.C.'s passionate lovemaking. Her choice was made.

"It's not what you think, J.C." After the words were out of her mouth she realized how shallow she sounded. That was the same line everyone used when they were caught with their hand in the cookie jar.

J.C. picked up Samantha's blouse and tossed it to her. "It's none of my business. I don't really give a damn what either of you do." Her lower lip trembled. "I'll see you in the morning," she said quietly as she quickly left the room her eyes overflowing with tears that spilled down her pale cheeks.

"I'd better talk to her, Ted." Samantha put on her blouse.

"I'm sorry, Samantha. I shouldn't have—"

"Ted, it's not your fault," she interrupted.

"If you need me to help talk to her, I'll be here," he offered.

She kissed his cheek. "Thank you."

Samantha tapped on J.C.'s door. She waited for a few seconds, then walked into the room and over to the bed where J.C. was sprawled. "J.C.," she said, touching her shoulder. She was silent, her face buried in her arms.

Samantha put her arms around J.C.'s shoulders, and when she looked down her gaze fell upon the opened but empty whiskey bottle. "J.C.!" she cried. "How could you? How long have you been drinking?"

"Leave me alone!"

"You aren't supposed to drink. That is the number one condition of your bail. How can you be so stupid?" she shouted.

"I said leave me alone, Samantha!" J.C. screamed as she pulled herself into a sitting position. She stared blankly at the wall.

"J.C., I think you and I need to have a talk."

"Go to hell!"

* * *

Samantha handed the empty bottle to Ted. "She won't talk to me."

"I didn't think she would." He shook his head. "She was doing so well lately, not even talking about drinking. And her friendship with Jo seemed to be helping her. I thought the worst was over."

"What do we do now?" she asked.

"I think we should just let her sleep it off tonight and try to talk to her in the morning."

"All right, Ted." She touched his shoulder. "I'm going to sleep in her room and keep an eye on her. Just in case she gets sick."

"I could stay over and sleep on the sofa."

"Maybe that would be a good idea. I'll get you some bedding."

He wondered what would happen when she slipped into bed with J.C. He tried to chase the thought from his mind, but couldn't. Images of them together played through his mind.

Samantha came back with the bedding. "Would you like me to make up the sofa for you?"

"No, I can do it," he said with a smile. "I'll see you in the morning." He kissed her cheek.

Samantha closed the bedroom door, then removed her clothing, leaving her underclothes on. J.C. was on the far side of the bed, fully clothed. Samantha so desperately wanted to touch her, and she knew deep within her soul that J.C. was fighting her own urges. She knew she wasn't asleep even though she pretended to be. She had to get her to talk; she couldn't let her slip back into her old drinking habits. "Why did you do it?" she whispered.

J.C. kept silent.

Samantha moved closer, but J.C. pushed her away. "Why are you here? Go to your own bed."

"I'm not leaving you alone tonight," she said softly. "Why did you drink, J.C.?"

She rolled over and faced her. "I didn't. I wanted to, but I couldn't. I poured the whiskey down the drain." She took a ragged breath then gazed deeply into Samantha's eyes. "It doesn't matter if you believe me or not, because I know I didn't do it."

The tone of her voice was so sincere that Samantha knew she was telling the truth. "I do believe you, J.C."

"I thought I could deal with you and Ted, but I can't. It hurts too much. Christy couldn't make it tonight and I didn't feel like keeping Jo out late again, so I came home early. When I saw you and Ted . . . I hope it was what you wanted." She lowered her eyes. "I won't drink—you're not worth it. I went through hell for my sobriety and I won't give it up because of you."

Samantha flinched at her words, but it was a mask J.C. hid behind to hide her pain. She could see it when she looked into those dark, haunted eyes. "Nothing happened. I couldn't have gone through with it even if you hadn't walked in on us," she said gently.

J.C. swallowed the lump in her throat. "Don't explain, Sam. It probably would have happened. I just got home too soon."

"No," she whispered. "I was thinking of you while he was touching me. It's you I want, J.C. It always has been, but I was a fool." She pressed her lips to J.C.'s. When she got no response, she tried to force her tongue inside J.C.'s mouth.

J.C. pushed her away. "Don't! I can't go on like this anymore. I'm going to explode! When you're certain that it's me you want and can give me a commitment, then I'll be here. I can't take anymore of these back and forth games."

"You do want me, J.C. I can feel it."

"More than you'll ever know," J.C. choked.

"Then be with me now," Samantha pleaded.

"Not until you can give me a commitment."

"Let's go on like we were. It'll be better now that you're not drinking."

55-DRON

"Do you still want only me?"

"That's not fair, J.C. I didn't sleep with Ted. That should answer your question."

"You were both naked. Would you have done it with him?"

"I didn't feel any desire for him."

"But would you have gone through with it if I hadn't walked in?"

"I don't know."

"I can't be with you, then," she said, turning her back to her.

The following morning J.C. walked into the kitchen, where Ted and Samantha were having coffee. "I need to talk to both of you. Please hear me out. I'll try to explain last night to you, but I don't think you'll ever understand." She poured herself a cup of coffee. "I wanted to drink that bottle. I wanted to blot out all of the hurts and fears inside of me, but I couldn't go through with it. I know that I have to face reality no matter how much I suffer. Taking that drink would've only been a temporary escape. I've learned that things will only get tougher for me if I continue to drink. This might not make sense to you, but I'm scared and I want to make something decent out of my life." She looked at Samantha. "There have been so many times I wanted to tell you what was going on deep inside of me, but instead of talking I would take a drink. Then the need to tell you would disappear."

"I was surprised to find out about Jo. She's been a very special and important part of your life and you never shared that with me."

J.C. sighed. "Jo and I are two of a kind. We met back when we were fourteen and discovered our sexuality together. We've had an on-again, off-again relationship through the years, but our friendship has always remained intact."

"Why didn't you ever tell me about her?"

"A long time ago I did. Only I never told you her name or about our friendship." J.C. sat down. "She was the only good thing that ever happened in my life. I didn't want to share that part of me with anyone."

"But didn't that hurt her that you shut her out during the years we were together?" Samantha asked.

"I suppose. But that's the way we have always been. If she were in a relationship, then I would stay away from her. But we would always be there for one another if the need arose."

"Why couldn't you have just introduced her to me and explained that she was from your past?"

She shook her head. "I don't know. It's just the way we are. I love her deeply, but it's not the same type of love. We could probably spend our lives together, but a part of me would yearn for something more."

"Is there more from your past, J.C.? I do care about everything that has happened to you," Samantha said.

"It's long and complicated." She toyed with the cross she wore around her neck. "We've been together all these years, Samantha, and it's about time you were introduced to the real me."

"Do you want me to leave?" Ted asked.

"No, I don't have anything to hide anymore."

"Well, we've got all day," he said.

"I come from a large family. I was born and raised here in the city. Most of my family still lives here, but I've managed to avoid them for the past ten years. Anyway, my childhood was like a nightmare. The minute I discovered alcohol, I could get away from the whole stinking bunch of them!" she said bitterly.

"What happened to you when you were a child, J.C.?" Ted asked.

She stared into her coffee cup. "I was raped by a close family friend when I was eight years old."

"Oh my God," Samantha murmured.

"Was the man ever charged for the crime?"

She stared at the table, absently running her fingernail back and forth over the surface. "No," she answered flatly. "My mother was very fond of him. She insinuated that I must have enticed him or else he wouldn't have touched me. My God, I was only a little kid! What the hell did I know about sex? Anyway, I was introduced to alcohol, and I found out that if I drank enough I wouldn't have to remember anymore and the nightmares would go away. At least for a little while they would. Then I started drinking more and more—whenever I could get it." She stood up and angrily rammed her hands into her jeans pockets. "My so-called brothers and sisters never gave a damn about me. They only used, then abused me. I had to be tougher than they were. I came and went when I pleased. That was my existence. But I did have dreams. My dreams kept me alive." She sighed.

"Ever since I was a kid, I was attracted to my same sex. Most of my friends would be drooling over the hunky new math teacher, trying to get him to notice them, while I was secretly lusting after the new English teacher, trying to keep my mind on the lesson and my eyes off her legs." She laughed sourly. "I dated once in a while, but it was only a cover. I wanted women. I craved them, but I couldn't tell anyone. I knew that no one would ever understand. It caused a deep void inside of me because I couldn't have what I truly wanted. I tried to convince myself that it would pass, but it didn't. Then when I was fourteen, Jo came into my life." She smiled. "Jo was my rock. She understood everything I was going through because she felt the same way about life that I did. You know the rest of my past with Jo."

"Were you in any other long term relationships besides Jo and Samantha?" Ted questioned.

She lowered her eyes again. "Yes, when I was eighteen. I was devastated when Jo told me she was going east to some fancy college. I didn't know what I was going to do without her. We'd been almost inseparable for the past four years. I felt that emptiness creeping up on me again. I didn't think I could survive without her, but I had no choice." She stared into Samantha's eyes. "I thought Jo and I were going to be together forever. I dreamed of us getting a place together and living happily ever after, but that wasn't meant to be. Those were just foolish kid dreams. I met an older woman, but it ended after a couple of years."

"What happened?" Ted asked.

J.C. stared ahead, not really looking at either of them. She didn't know if she could relive that painful part of her past again, but she needed to get it off her chest. "Jody was her name. She'd been divorced for a few years and had a couple of kids. No one knew she was gay. She was a big shot executive, and she used to come into Harve's to pick up women and one night she picked me up. She liked me, so after a while she invited me to move into her condo with her. Since she had kids, I was known as the live-in nanny to her neighbors and associates. She said no one could ever know that we were lovers." She looked in Samantha's direction, and she read the guilt in Samantha's eyes.

J.C. sipped at her coffee. "Anyway," she continued, "one night we had an argument, and I told her that I was leaving for good. She started to cry and told me how much she needed me and how the kids were attached to me. I explained to her that her kids weren't my responsibility. All I ever did was baby-sit. We never went anywhere together, because she was either in meetings or socializing with other executives. She couldn't very well bring the nanny with her, and of course, I was a woman." She inhaled deeply, then slowly let her breath out. "She gave me everything money could buy, but I needed more out of life. I wanted to have fun. I felt like I was suffocating. I was still a kid and she was almost forty."

Samantha's eyes widened, but she kept silent.

"She asked me to take the kids out for ice cream and spend some time with them before I left. She wanted me to tell them that I was leaving. I really did love those kids." Tears filled her eyes. "She knew that I loved them and she used them to get me to stay. I didn't want to take them anywhere because I had been drinking too much that night." She lowered her eyes again. "I kept telling her that it was a bad idea for me to take them, but she kept insisting."

"What happened?" Ted asked.

"She gave me the car keys, so I gave in to her like I always did." She cleared her throat. "I don't know much else after that. Just

55-DRON

what I was later told. I ended up in the hospital." Her eyes brimmed with tears. "I should have died, not the kids," she said in a strangled voice. Samantha's hand flew to her mouth.

"J.C., I know this is hard, but try," Ted prompted.

"I asked the doctor about the kids. He looked at me like he despised me—I'll never forget that look on his face for as long as I live. I kept asking him over and over, and finally he told me that I hit another car head on. The people in the other car weren't seriously injured, but the kids had rolled off the back seat." She couldn't swallow the lump in her throat. "All I could say was that I was sorry,' she sobbed. "I was so sorry. I did love those kids."

Samantha walked over to her and threw her arms around J.C.'s neck. "I didn't know." Tears streamed down her cheeks. "Why didn't you tell me?"

"J.C., I think after awhile you'll be glad that you were able to get all of this out in the open. I can't imagine the turmoil you went through." He patted her hands. "Did Jo ever know about this?"

She sniffed. "Yes. But we promised each other that we would never discuss it. Jo and I kept in touch regularly and I flew to visit her at college a couple of times. She never liked Jody. She thought that Jody was using me, but she never interfered. When I was in the hospital, she took a semester off from college and stayed with me the whole time."

"It's a good thing you had her in your life, J.C. She's a wonderful woman."

"Yes, she is," she whispered.

Ted looked at the two women. "I should go. I think you two have a lot to talk about."

Samantha nodded.

"I'll see myself out," he said.

"Thanks, Ted," she answered.

Samantha poured two fresh cups of coffee. "I wish you would have told me all of this before, J.C. Maybe I could've understood more about your drinking."

"Don't you get it, Sam?" J.C. pounded her fist on the table. "My drinking brought misery, not only to myself but to everyone around me. The more suffering it caused, the more I drank. I can't undo the past." She gazed at Samantha through tear-swollen eyes. "Look what it did to us."

"But, J.C., you know how I feel about you."

"Let's just be friends, Sam. Let me get through this trial and then I'll get out of your life for good. I've seriously been considering leaving the city and making a fresh start somewhere else. I have nothing left here."

"What about Jo?"

"She's trying to work things out with her girlfriend. Besides, Jo and I will always be there for each other. I have to start depending on just myself for once in my life."

"Then what about me, dammit! You have me."

J.C. shook her head. "I can't share you."

"You don't have to. How can I convince you of that?"

J.C. let out a ragged breath. "I can't talk about this anymore. Let's just go on like we have these past few months . . . just until the trial is over. We both need to think about our futures."

"I can't imagine you not being in my life," Samantha said tearfully.

"You'll always be in my heart, Sam," she said softly.

Two hours later J.C. walked into the living room.

"Where are you going, J.C.?" Samantha asked.

"To a meeting. Jo will be here in half an hour."

"We need to talk about us, J.C."

She flashed her a weak smile. "I'll be okay, Sam. Hey, I've hit rock bottom, so now the only way is up. I'll make it."

"I know you will, but I want us to make it together."

"I wish I could truly believe that, Sam."

The doorbell sounded. "Maybe Jo's early," she called, running to the door. "Hi, Ted, Samantha's in the living room. Go on in. I have to meet Jo in the lobby."

Ted placed a hand firmly on her shoulder. "The court date has been set, J.C."

Her heart lurched. "When?"

"Monday."

She felt weak. "That's too soon."

Samantha hurried to the entrance hall. "What's going on?" she fearfully asked.

"The court date has been set for Monday," Ted explained.

Samantha searched his face. "Are you prepared, Ted?"

"I tried to stall for another week, but it was a no go. At this point, we're as prepared as we can be."

"Let's sit down and discuss this," Samantha said, leading the way into the living room.

"J.C., please don't worry. The prosecution doesn't have anything solid to convict you on," Ted assured her.

"Then why was I charged in the first place and bail set so high?"

He scratched his cheek.

"They must have something. If only I could remember," she moaned. "Dammit!"

"Calm down. You need to stay sharp and alert. We'll get through this."

The doorbell sounded again.

"It must be Jo," J.C. said.

"I'll get it," Samantha offered.

A few seconds later Samantha and Jo walked into the living room. Jo ran over to J.C., throwing her arms around her neck. "It'll be all right," she soothed.

Samantha wanted to be the one giving comfort to her but knew that J.C. wouldn't allow it. She ached to pull her into her arms and assure her that everything would be okay, and that they would start their lives anew once this was behind them. That was what she truly wanted, but convincing J.C. of it was another obstacle—one she wasn't sure she could move.

"I think you need to get to as many meetings as you can, honey," Jo said. "All our friends are behind you."

J.C. numbly nodded.

"J.C., could I please speak to you privately for just a moment?"

"Sure." She followed Samantha into the kitchen.

Samantha laid a hand on her shoulder as her eyes searched J.C.'s. "J.C., I love you. What can I do to convince you of that? Please tell me what to do."

J.C. looked at her tear-filled eyes. "Did you tell Ted that you and he are only friends and that you've made your choice?"

"No, I . . ."

"Then you really aren't sure what you want." She threw her hands up. "Nothing's changed, Sam. I'm not playing games anymore."

"I'll tell him. I promise . . . tonight."

"No, Sam. I'm tired of always being second best. I've got too much going on right now. Please don't put this pressure on me. I don't know how much more I can take," she said in a shaky voice.

Samantha watched her leave the room. She had to find a way to convince her that she wanted only her. She needed to tell Ted, but the timing was wrong. J.C.'s case was too important. Ted didn't need to be burdened right now, just as J.C. didn't. She would have to wait for the right moment.

* * *

J.C. nervously looked around the crowded courtroom. She caught Samantha's eye, and Samantha smiled reassuringly at her. Jo was seated a few rows behind Samantha. She winked and gave her the thumbs up. J.C. watched Ted hurry into the room and quickly seat himself beside her. He grabbed her arm. "Don't worry. It's going to be all right. Do you trust me?"

She nodded.

"Good." He smiled.

Her heart thumped when the judge entered the courtroom. Her legs shook as she stood up, and she was relieved when everyone sat back down. Her mind was a blur as she focused on Stuart Brewster's opening statement to the court.

55-DRON

He walked back and forth in front of the jury box. "What I have to say is going to be brief, ladies and gentlemen," he stated. "But at the conclusion of this trial, I am positive that you will be convinced that in the early morning hours of March 11, Joyce Markin murdered Harvey Barthow. Why did she commit such an act of violence? For a cheap bottle of whiskey! His friends and patrons of the small tavern he owned and operated for over thirty years respected Harvey Barthow. He was a kind, gentle, friendly man. He was a man willing to help a friend in need. Joyce Markin was said to have been like a daughter to him. Now examine the background of Joyce Markin. She's never held a steady job. She has numerous arrests for petit larceny, assault, unlawful possession of a controlled substance, and a number of other offenses. The question is why? Why did she commit murder for a bottle of whiskey? The defense will try to convince you that she never committed this crime—that she was framed. Listen to the evidence as it is presented in this case. I am confident that you will come to the conclusion, beyond a shadow of a doubt, that Joyce Markin is a detriment to society and that you will reach a verdict of guilty in the first degree." He paused for a moment. "Thank you."

"Counsel for the defense, you may give your opening statement to the court," the judge ordered.

"Thank you, Your Honor." Ted stood in front of the defendants' table. "Ladies and gentlemen, my statement to you this morning will also be brief. When this trial concludes, I am assured that you will agree that Joyce Markin was framed. It was easy for someone to frame her. Who was that someone? Someone with a deep hatred for her. Someone with a personal grudge against Joyce Markin murdered Harvey Barthow, then left her to take the punishment for a crime she never committed. Joyce Markin is a survivor. She learned at a young age how to survive on her own. Her one true friend was a man named Harvey Barthow. He was the father she never had. She loved and respected him.

"Joyce Markin has a disease called alcoholism and is in recovery. For several months she has been rehabilitating herself. Listen to all of the testimony. Keep an open mind. I am confident that you will come to the conclusion that Joyce Markin did not commit murder on March 11. Thank you." He returned to his seat.

J.C. tried to keep her mind focused, but she had missed much of both opening statements. Her mind drifted to the last time she had seen Harve. Why couldn't she remember? The frustration gnawed at her. But she had to center her mind on the trial. She cautiously watched as the first witness for the prosecution was sworn in.

"Please tell the court what you saw in the early morning hours of March 11, Mrs. Sargeant," Stuart Brewster said.

"I heard someone knocking on Mr. Barthow's door. I looked out of my door and saw that young woman standing in the hall," the elderly woman said, wagging a finger in J.C.'s direction. "I looked at my clock. It was exactly fifteen minutes after three. I closed the door, then I got myself a glass of milk and when I returned, the woman was gone. Everything was quiet and I sat in my living room for a few minutes, but I didn't hear anything."

"You are certain that this is the woman you saw outside of Harvey Barthow's apartment." He stood in front of J.C..

J.C. looked at the woman's tired, worn face. She had never seen her before, but then, in Harve's building, the majority of the tenants kept themselves barricaded behind locked doors most of the time, only venturing out into the world when the need arose.

"That's the woman I saw," Mrs. Sargeant said emphatically.

"I have no further questions," Stuart Brewster said.

"Does the defense have any questions for this witness?" Judge Koviac asked.

"Yes, Your Honor," Ted said as he walked to the witness box, placing a hand on the rail. He looked first at the jury, then at the witness. "Mrs. Sargeant, you did not see Joyce Markin actually entering or leaving Harvey Barthow's apartment, did you?"

She eyed him suspiciously. "I saw her knocking on his door."

"But you didn't see Harvey Barthow open the door to let her in, did you?"

"No, I didn't."

"How do you know that Joyce Markin didn't leave the building during the time you went to get a glass of milk?" he asked.

"After I closed my door, I immediately went to the window. It overlooks the street. I didn't see anyone in either direction. She couldn't have left that quickly."

Ted frowned. "I have no further questions for you at this time, Mrs. Sargeant, but I may recall you later."

"You may step down," Judge Koviac said. "Would the prosecution call your next witness?"

"I'd like to call Darcy Sebastion to the stand," Stuart Brewster said.

J.C. wondered what Darcy would have to say about her. In any event, whatever Darcy said wouldn't be in her favor. It was evident from the first day they met that Darcy didn't like her. She watched as Darcy confidently made her way to the witness stand, heels clicking on the floor. She smiled widely as she was sworn in. J.C. caught her eye but broke the intense glare Darcy directed at her.

Brewster paced in front of the witness stand for a few seconds, then turned abruptly to face his witness. "Mrs. Sebastion, how long have you known the defendant, Joyce Markin?"

Darcy looked at J.C. When J.C. didn't raise her eyes, she looked at her questioner. "I have known J.C—that's her nickname—for approximately five years." She smoothed her knit skirt over her knees.

"If you had to describe Joyce Markin, what would your description of her character be?"

"I object!" Ted angrily shouted, jumping to his feet.

"I see nothing intimidating about the question, Counselor," the judge firmly said. "Objection overruled." He turned to Darcy. "You may answer the question."

Ted sat down, clearly infuriated. He had no grounds to call for an objection, but J.C. knew he needed time. He rolled a pencil back and forth in the palm of his hand as he awaited Darcy's reply.

Darcy flashed the judge a bright smile. "J.C. Markin is a self-centered woman. She is incapable of caring about anyone but herself. From the first day I met her, she has brought nothing but pain and sorrow to those around her. She is an arrogant, uneducated hustler who—"

"Objection!" Ted again shouted.

"Objection sustained," Judge Koviac ruled. "Please instruct your witness to answer the question knowledgeably, without adding her own suppositions," he stated, sharply eyeing Brewster.

"Mrs. Sebastion," Brewster said, walking over to the jury box. He placed his hand on the rail, then turned to face Darcy. "How did you become acquainted with Joyce Markin?"

Darcy took a deep breath. "A friend of mine, Samantha Wheeler, introduced me to her."

"I see. And you and Samantha Wheeler have been friends for a long period of time?"

"Yes," she answered, nodding her head. "Our families were in the same social circles, consequently attending many of the same social functions. We shared the same circle of friends."

"So it surprised you when Samantha Wheeler began this friendship with Joyce Markin, who was evidently not in your social ranking. Is my assumption correct?"

"Yes. Samantha had been suffering because of some tragic losses in her life. I believed that it was just a phase and she would come to her senses."

Brewster walked over to her. "Why do you have such a dislike for Joyce Markin?"

Darcy's eyes flashed angrily. "She's a dyke," she spat out.

"Objection!"

"Objection sustained."

J.C. felt her face flush and wished she could turn around to see Samantha's reaction, but Ted had instructed her to never turn to look at the spectators.

"Thank you, Mrs. Sebastion. I have no further questions for you at this time, but I will recall you at a later time."

Ted wondered what Brewster was up to. He had to tread cautiously. As he slowly stood up he stared at Darcy, despising her. He looked sharply into her eyes as he moved towards her. "Mrs. Sebastion," he began, "why would a woman of your so-called 'social status' inhabit a bar such as Harve's when it is so obviously far removed from the social clubs you normally attend?"

"Samantha was in awe of the place. So, out of curiosity, I went there with her one night. It's nice to see how the other half lives," she stated coolly, keeping pace with Ted's eyes boring into her own.

"I don't understand. Why did you keep returning to Harve's Bar? After your curiosity was satisfied, why keep going back? What was the attraction?" He waited for a moment, then continued, "You knew that it was a gay bar, didn't you?"

His question caught her off guard; her face turned crimson. "I . . . I don't know. The atmosphere, I suppose, is why I kept going back," she answered nervously, avoiding his eyes.

"Were you acquainted with the deceased, Harvey Barthow?"

"Yes, of course I was. He was a very charming man, friendly to all of his patrons. He made it a point to get to know all of the regulars and gave the bar a homey atmosphere."

"So, then, you became a regular?"

"No—I," she stuttered. "I went several times, so I assume that he must have thought I was becoming a regular."

"I see." He paced in front of her for a few seconds, then put a finger to his brow. "How was your friendship with Samantha Wheeler affected by her friendship with Joyce Markin?"

Darcy cleared her throat. "Samantha was verbally and emotionally abused by J.C. I tried to reason with Samantha about the evident mistreatment, but she refused to listen. I can't stand to see the ill treatment, so I've been avoiding Samantha. J.C. just doesn't fit into our world and never will, no matter how much Samantha would like her to."

"What has Joyce Markin done to you personally to cause you so much bitterness towards her?"

"It's rather involved."

"Go ahead," Ted prompted.

She narrowed her eyes. "Eventually Samantha ended her friendship with J.C. and we were becoming close again. We were renewing our friendship, and it felt good to go to our old clubs together once again. Things seemed to be getting back to normal, until one night when J.C. showed up. Without provocation J.C. attacked Samantha out of, what I assume, was a jealous rage."

"Does Joyce Markin's sexual preference for women bother you?"

"I don't care who she sleeps with, Mr. Jamison, if that is what you are implying."

"Was Samantha Wheeler having an affair with Joyce Markin?"

"Yes."

A murmur echoed throughout the room. "Order!" Judge Koviac demanded.

"Did this upset you?" Ted asked.

Darcy wrung her hands. "Yes. Samantha had always shown a normal interest in men and this attraction to J.C. was difficult for me to accept. Friendship was one thing, but this was going too far. I'm positive that Samantha never realized what she was getting herself into when she became involved with J.C."

"Did you ever talk to Samantha Wheeler about her sexual involvement with Joyce Markin?" Ted continued to stare at her.

Darcy shifted uncomfortably in her seat. "Yes, but she would never divulge much. She was extremely protective of J.C."

Ted shifted his gaze to J.C., then back to Darcy. "Isn't it true, Mrs. Sebastion, that deep down inside you harbor sexual feelings for Samantha Wheeler yourself and that is the reason you despise Joyce Markin so intensely? She had the woman you've secretly desired for years!"

Whispers again resonated throughout the crowded room.

"Isn't it true, Mrs. Sebastion, that you kept going back to Harve's Bar to satisfy your own sexual cravings?"

"No!" Darcy screamed. "I'm not that type of person!"

J.C. watched Darcy. She was surprised that Brewster hadn't objected. She stole a glance at him; he was perfectly composed, listening intently.

"You were jealous of Joyce Markin's affair with the woman you loved!" Ted's voice boomed. "Isn't that the truth, Mrs. Sebastion? Your thoughts of them together were more than you could bear. It consumed you!"

"I—No! Maybe! I thought about it, but I knew it would never happen. It's perfectly normal to fantasize about the same sex!" she cried.

"I have no further questions, Your Honor," Ted said, smiling at Darcy.

"You may step down," Judge Koviac said. "Please call the next witness," he said, focusing on the prosocuter.

"I'd like to call Samantha Wheeler to the stand."

J.C. closely watched as Samantha was sworn in. Her golden hair glistened against the navy two-piece suit she wore. She was stylish, with just enough jewelry to accent her outfit. But J.C. felt sorry for her because now everyone knew about their affair. She had brought humiliation, when all she had ever wanted was to bring happiness to Samantha. She longed to reach out and hold her, just for a moment. How could she explain to a prejudiced world that the love they shared had not been a sick, deviate act, but was as pure as any love could be? What they had once shared would now only remain etched forever in her memory, but Samantha would forever remain her one and only true love.

Brewster stood menacingly in front of the witness stand. He looked into Samantha's eyes. "Miss Wheeler, do you admit to having had a sexual relationship with the defendant, Joyce Markin?"

"Yes, I do", she answered calmly.

"Can you describe for the court what effect alcohol had on Joyce Markin?"

"When J.C. drank, she could become verbally abusive or become very hard on herself."

"Were you abused by her as stated in previous testimony from Darcy Sebastion?"

"Yes, I was on occasion verbally abused, but that is not J.C.'s normal behavior. She is a very loving, caring person, incapable of hurting anyone physically."

"Until the night she caused injury to yourself?"

"That was the only time and it was an accident."

"It only takes one time, Miss Wheeler, to set up a pattern of abuse. Maybe what you perceive as an accident wasn't perceived the same way by a bystander."

"J.C. knew that her alcohol abuse was the root of her problems, and she has been faithfully attending Alcoholics Anonymous."

J.C. caught Samantha's eye and smiled.

"How could you maintain a personal relationship with this woman after you were abused by her?"

"That wasn't J.C., not the J.C. I knew and loved. I know she never intended to hurt me."

"Why did you post bail and invite Joyce Markin to live in your home while she awaited her trial?"

"She's my friend, and I would do anything humanly possible to help her. The charge against her is absurd!" She looked pointedly at him. "She worshipped Harvey."

"But you stated a moment ago that she wasn't herself when she abused you."

"Yes, I did, but that doesn't mean she would commit murder. That's quite a difference."

"You heard Darcy Sebastion's testimony?"

"Yes."

"In all the years you and Darcy Sebastion socialized, did you ever once suspect that her feelings for you were more than that of friendship?"

"No, I did not."

"I have no further questions for this witness at this time, Your Honor," Brewster abruptly stated.

"Would you care to cross-examine?" the judge asked Ted.

55-DRON

"Not at this time, Your Honor."

"Very well then. This court will be adjourned until nine o'clock tomorrow morning."

* * *

Samantha smiled at J.C. as she made her way back to her seat. A burden had been lifted from her shoulders; it didn't matter what anyone thought about her anymore. She was out in the open. There was no more hiding, and she had to convince J.C. that she had made her choice. After the trial she would explain her feelings to Ted, and then she and J.C. could live their lives without having to worry about who would find out.

CHAPTER SEVEN

"Calm down, J.C. Everything is going our way." Ted patted her shoulder. "You'll most likely be called to testify tomorrow. Try to get some rest."

"Do you want to catch a meeting tonight?" Jo asked, slipping an arm through J.C.'s.

"I think I'd better," J.C. answered tiredly.

"Do you think that's a good idea?" Samantha motioned to the swarm of reporters converging on them, cameras flashing in their faces.

"I'll take good care of her," Jo promised, whisking her through the crowd to Samantha's car.

Ted followed, escorting Samantha to her car and refusing to comment as the reporters thrust microphones at him. "I'll stop by this evening," he promised.

"I'm sorry, Sam," J.C. said once they were safely inside the apartment.

"No, J.C., it's not your fault. Ted told us to expect this." She smiled. "You held up very well, and I am so proud of you."

"I couldn't do anything but sit there and listen." She searched Samantha's face. "I'm sorry that our relationship had to be brought out into the open."

Samantha gently squeezed her arm. "I'm relieved that it is. I don't have to worry about anyone finding out anymore. Besides, no one forced me to have a relationship with you; it was my choice."

"I don't know what I'd do without you, baby," J.C. said softly, barely realizing she had uttered her favorite term of endearment for Samantha.

"It's been so long since you've called me that."

J.C. swallowed hard. "I'm sorry . . . I wasn't thinking."

"It's okay. I loved when you called me that. I always have." She put her arms around J.C., drawing her close, then stroked her hair. "How can I convince you that I love you? I need you, J.C.," she whispered.

J.C. sighed. She yearned for Samantha's touch and wished that she never had to relinquish her embrace, but she had to. She would be leaving Samantha for good just as soon as the trial was over, and any physical contact between them now would only add to her anguish. She summoned her faltering willpower and pulled away, then looked deeply into Samantha's eyes. "I wonder if you've ever truly known the depth of my love for you."

"I do, J.C. I was wrong. I've been trying to tell you for weeks now, honey, but you won't believe me."

"I've got to get ready for my meeting, because Jo's taking me to dinner first. What time is Ted coming over?"

"Eight o'clock."

"Okay, well, I'm going to get ready." She started to walk out of the room when Samantha grabbed her arm.

"We haven't finished talking."

J.C. looked into the beautiful, glistening eyes that danced with excitement.

"I have something important to tell you."

"Have you told Ted you're not interested in him sexually?" J.C. asked pointedly

"No, but . . ."

"We can talk tomorrow." She pulled away from Samantha's grasp. "I just can't listen to anymore talking right now."

Samantha watched her walk away. Ted needed to be told tonight. She couldn't back down. J.C. was too important to her, and she wasn't going to risk losing her for good. Ted was a mature man, certainly capable of keeping his persnonal emotions in check as far as J.C.'s case was concerned. Her reluctance in not telling him sooner had only been an excuse to forestall what she'd known for a long time—a woman was what she wanted and desired, but not just any woman. It was J.C. It had always been J.C., but how could she ever convince her of that fact now? J.C. would only think she was using her for a moment of gratifying sexual pleasure. All she knew for certain was that tonight she intended to have the love she truly longed for and craved. She would prove to J.C. once and for all that the indecision and uncertainty was in the past. She was ready to commit herself to her one and only true love.

* * *

Stu Brewster smiled smugly as he loosened his tie. "I believe I've got this case all wrapped up, Ted. There is no way in hell you're going to prove Joyce Markin's innocence."

"Don't count your win yet, Stu. You may be surprised at the outcome of tomorrow's testimony," he said, removing his suit coat.

Brewster leaned forward in his chair. "Don't play games with me, Ted. Joyce Markin doesn't have many friends. She's going to be convicted for murder." He took a long swallow from his drink. "You have surprised me, though, by putting Joyce Markin on the stand tomorrow."

"I want the jury to see her as a real person. I want them to become familiar with the human side of her."

Stu laughed. "I'll break her down piece by piece until she crumbles."

Ted's eyes narrowed, but he let the remark pass. "I was surprised that you didn't object during my cross-examination of Darcy Sebastion."

"I'll level with you on that one, Ted. I don't like the woman's attitude and didn't mind seeing her knocked down a peg or two."

He nodded. "But I don't see where your certainty in a conviction is coming from. I haven't seen any concrete evidence being brought forward that can possibly prove that Joyce Markin stabbed Barthow."

"No one else had a motive, and she was seen at the apartment." He sighed tiredly, putting his elbows on the table as he squinted at Ted. "Now, you wouldn't happen to have any surprises up your sleeve, would you?" he asked gruffly, peering into the younger man's face.

Ted's eyes twinkled mischievously. "I've got to go, Stu. I'll see you in court in the morning."

Twenty minutes later he sat in Samantha's living room. "I think I know what you want to tell me, Samantha," he said. "You really want to be with J.C., don't you? I've known it for quite some time now."

Samantha was grateful for the understanding and acceptance in his voice as she took his hand in hers. "I don't expect you to understand this love, but I have finally realized that what I shared with J.C. is the love I want for the rest of my life." Her face flushed. "That's why I couldn't make love with you. It felt wrong, unnatural. I'm so sorry if I've led you on or hurt you. I never meant to."

"No," he said gently, squeezing her hand. "You've been nothing but honest with me. I was the one who pushed you. All I want is your happiness. Now if you would have chosen another guy over me, then that might be a different story," he teased.

"Thank you." Her eyes brimmed with tears.

He smiled. "Just be happy."

"I am, Ted. J.C. gives me a reason for living. She has from the moment I met her."

"I still want to be a part of your life, though. But as a friend."

"Always," she promised.

* * *

J.C. was silent through the meeting. Jo sat at her side, every now and then giving her hand a reassuring squeeze. She tried to concentrate on what was being said but could barely comprehend the topic. Tomorrow she had to convince the jury of her innocence. An intense loneliness engulfed her. Whenever she was away from Samantha, she felt as though a part of herself was missing. Her heart had been severed. She could hardly stand being so close to her night after night, living in her home, aching to touch her, but knowing that she couldn't. The trial would soon be over, and she would either be going to prison or leaving the city. In either case, she would be apart from her only true love. She blinked back tears. She didn't know how she would ever get through this night especially knowing that Samantha was probably in Ted's arms at this very moment. She couldn't bear to spend another long night alone. Tomorrow her fate could very well be sealed, and she needed to enjoy what might be her last few weeks of freedom.

When the meeting ended, she stood by Jo's side, talking with a few women when Christy and Mark joined her.

"We're here for you," Mark said with loyalty in his voice.

She smiled. "It's nice to have friends."

"We've always been here, and we always will be. Just hang in there, and everything will turn out all right," Christy said, and then gave her a hug. "I'll be waiting for your call tomorrow night."

J.C. nodded numbly.

"Do you want to talk for awhile?" Jo asked.

"Thank you, Jo." She squeezed her hand. "I don't know what I'd do without you right now."

"That's what being a friend is all about . . . almost like marriage, when you think about it—in the good times as well as the bad times." She flashed a bright smile. "There's nothing I wouldn't do for you, J.C. We've been through too much together." They silently walked to Jo's car and got inside. Jo put the key in the ignition.

"Can you wait a minute before starting the car, Jo?"

"Sure. Are you all right?"

"I—I—" she whimpered. "I'm sorry," she choked.

Jo scooped her into her arms. "It's going to be all right, J.C. I'll see you through this." She rubbed her back, slowly rocking J.C. in her arms.

J.C.'s shoulders heaved. "I . . . I hurt so badly, Jo," she sniffed.

"I know," she soothed. "I really think you need to give Samantha more time, honey. She really cares about you."

35-DRON

"Then why the games?"

"I can't answer that. She needs to be certain, and if her choice is Ted, then you'll let her go, but until you know for sure don't give up hope."

J.C. sniffed again. "I know you're right," she said, dabbing at her eyes with the tissue Jo had placed in her hand.

"Where's Samantha tonight?"

"With Ted."

Jo was silent for a minute. "Do you want to get some coffee or something to eat?"

J.C. stared at her friend for a long minute, then impulsively pulled her close. Her lips found Jo's and she kissed her gently, feeling the fires of their past passion building within her until the kiss turned into an inferno of longing and need.

Gasping, Jo pushed her away. "J.C., are you certain?" Her eyes searched J.C.'s for assurance.

J.C. nodded. "Come home with me. Spend the night with me, Jo. I need you."

Jo coughed nervously. "I feel like a teenager again. It's been so long since you and I . . ."

J.C. let her breath out slowly. "I'm sorry. I have no right. I would never use you like that, Jo." Her eyes pleaded with Jo's for understanding. "You believe me, don't you?"

"Of course I do. Our lovemaking isn't wrong, J.C. We've always been there for one another in every aspect. You remember our rule—if either of us is involved with another, then it's off limits, but since neither of us are in a committed relationship we're both free to do as we want."

"I do love you, Jo."

"And you know that sometimes my feelings for you run deeper in that area than yours do for me."

"But we've tried living together."

Jo laughed. "Yeah, we had fun, but I'd still rather have you for a friend than a full time partner."

J.C. grew serious. "Jo, do you think anyone would ever understand our relationship?"

She was thoughtful for a minute. "I don't know, but then I don't really care. We've always had something special together, J.C." She looked into her eyes. "I don't feel guilty or ashamed. If either of us were in a committed relationship, then yes, it would be wrong. It's not as though we're using one another." She leaned back in the seat. "I remember the first time you told me you had a crush on someone else. At first it hurt because we'd been together for three years, but then I thought about it and realized that you and I had something together which went much deeper than sex." She frowned. "I'm not explaining this very well."

"Yes, you are," J.C. answered as she ran her fingertips up Jo's stocking-clad leg. "We're safe, and we both know it just as we both know the depths of our passion for one another."

"Yes, I guess you could call it safe. But our love goes way beyond the sex, even though that has always been fantastic." She stopped J.C.'s roving hand. "If you continue, you know what's going to happen right here and now in the car."

J.C. saw the twinkle in her eye. "Let's go to my place," she whispered. "I need to be with you tonight. I need to hold and be held by you." She kissed her fervently.

Jo started the car, and they drove in silence with their hands entwined.

Once inside the darkened apartment J.C. realized that Samantha hadn't returned. "She's not home," she said. "Do you want something to drink?"

"No, I'm fine."

J.C. took Jo's hand and led her down the hall to her bedroom. She closed the door, then turned and took Jo into her arms. "You smell so nice," she whispered nuzzling her face in her silky hair.

Jo ran her fingerstips through J.C.'s hair, then tilted her head back as J.C.'s waiting lips met hers.

J.C.'s hands traveled to Jo's blouse, where she slowly unfastened the buttons, then gently slid it from Jo's back. She unhooked

5-DRON

the bra, letting it fall to the floor. Her hands cupped Jo's aching breasts. A moan escaped from her lips. She caressed Jo's smooth flesh and teased Jo's tongue with her own until their passion could be contained no longer. She led Jo to her bed, their lips never parting, and carefully eased her body down on top of Jo's, arching her back slightly so Jo could remove her panties. She enclosed Jo in her arms, luxuriating in the familiarity of her. She felt Jo moving beneath her, then shifted her weight as her hand traveled to Jo's waiting vagina. She softly inched her fingers inside, gently rubbing and massaging as the juices flowing from her stimulated J.C. She knew that Jo was on fire and needed release. She broke the kiss, then guided her tongue down Jo's chest, stopping to enjoy the taste of her firm breasts.

Jo's fingers were tangled in J.C.'s hair. "Now, baby, please take me now," Jo said in short raspy breaths.

J.C.'s tongue moved to Jo's stomach as she tenderly opened Jo's legs, moving closer to her treasure.

Later they lay entwined in one another's arms. J.C. listened to Jo's rhythmic breathing as she stroked Jo's hair, treasuring the passion they had just shared. She thought back to that night long ago when they had discovered one another. The recollection brought a smile to her lips.

J.C. had nervously placed her lips on Jo's. It felt so good and right. When her tongue met Jo's, a tingle rippled through her body, but the ache between her legs was so intense, she could barely move.

Jo fumbled with her clothes, but finally both of them had stood facing one another gazing at their nakedness. J.C.'s eyes traveled to Jo's crop of pubic auburn hair. She shyly touched it, seeing the sensation it brought to Jo. Jo's breath quickened as she touched J.C.'s dark thatch. J.C. slowly slid a finger into the opening, delighting in the wetness she found within.

"That feels good," Jo whispered.

J.C.'s lack of knowledge was replaced by the joy she had found in her friend's body. She continued moving her fingers until Jo could barely stand up.

They lay on the bed exploring one another. "I—I don't know what to do," J.C. whispered frantically.

"Just don't stop." Jo's voice was hoarse. "Continue what you're doing."

J.C.'s fingers dripped with Jo's juices.

"Don't stop," Jo moaned, then arched her back as she experienced her first climax. When she was finished, she stared deeply into J.C.'s eyes. "Let me do you."

J.C. was throbbing so intensely, she could barely speak.

"I want to try something different," Jo said, kissing J.C.'s stomach. "I want to taste you."

A shudder tore through J.C. when Jo's tongue entered her. Her fantasies couldn't compare to this reality. Explosions rocketed through her, ending in a breathless climax. Afterward they lay together, gently touching and feeling one another's bodies. Their raging fourteen-year-old hormones made them almost inseparable after that. J.C. agonized whenever she saw Jo in the high school hallway, wanting her but knowing she would have to wait until the final bell.

She smiled and held Jo closer, savoring the feel of her. With Jo she still felt the same passion she had at the age of fourteen. She closed her eyes, then drifted into a restless sleep. She barely heard the light tapping on her bedroom door; her eyes popped open when she noticed quiet tiptoeing across the carpet and toward the bed. The light from the window illuminated Samantha's naked body, causing J.C.'s heart to lurch. She winced as Samantha drew closer.

"I need to talk to you, J.C. I've been trying to all week, but you won't listen." Her words came in a rush. "I spent the past four hours talking to Ted. He understands that it's you I want." She sat on the edge of the bed and ran her fingertips over J.C.'s bare arm, then bent down to kiss J.C.'s cheek. "I want to be with you forever . . ." Her hand flew to her mouth. "Oh my God!" she choked, jumping to her feet. "I didn't know . . ."

"Sam, wait!" J.C. grabbed her arm, but Samantha wrestled out of her hold and ran sobbing from the room.

"Shit," J.C. mumbled, turning to Jo. "I'm sorry," she whispered.

"She loves you, J.C. Go to her."

J.C. swallowed the lump in her throat. "I don't know what to say."

Jo kissed her forehead. "You'll find the right words. You and Samantha have that special something together, J.C."

"Then why is it so hard?"

"That's what will make it endure."

"What about you, Jo?" she asked.

"I'll be where I've always been—making sure my best friend doesn't get hurt." She lit a cigarette, then slowly blew the smoke out. "Watching you and Samantha has made me think about what I've been putting Rachel through."

J.C. propped herself on an elbow. "And?"

"Sometimes I think I was trying too hard to keep the innocence of our youth," she answered thoughtfully. "It was safe with us because we didn't have to worry about walking away from one another. With or without the sex, we knew we would still be together. I've never really given Rachel a chance." She laughed. "Maybe it's time I settled down."

"Maybe it's time to give Rachel the commitment?"

She nodded. "Look what Samantha's lack of commitment has done to you."

"Do you truly love Rachel?"

"Yes, I do." She got out of bed, grabbed her clothes, and threw them on. "I'm going to tell her now—tonight." She put her arms around J.C. "Go to Samantha." She touched J.C.'s cheek. "I'll see you in court in the morning."

J.C. jumped into the shower, letting the hot water run down her back as she lathered her body with soap, then rinsed it off. She turned the water off and toweled herself dry. She didn't bother dressing, but hurried into Samantha's room.

"The games end tonight, Samantha," she said in a forceful voice, closing the door behind her. "I'm going to make this work—we're going to make this work."

Samantha was sprawled across her bed, shoulders heaving. J.C. climbed in next to her and pressed her body tightly to hers.

"Just go away, J.C.," she pleaded. "Go back to your girlfriend."

"Jo's not my girlfriend." She put her arms around Samantha. "We're good friends."

"It just happened? Is that what you expect me to believe?"

"Yes, it's the truth. Jo and I . . . we're just friends, and it happened because I couldn't stand the images of you and Ted together."

"I thought she had a girlfriend."

"Jo wasn't sure, but now she's ready to try with Rachel." She ran her hand through her damp hair. "You put me through hell! I imagined all sorts of things between you and Ted after I walked in on you that night. Do you know what that did to me?"

"I guess forever has a different meaning for you," Samantha sniffed.

"I don't believe what I'm hearing," J.C. retorted bitterly. "I'm the one who wanted forever; you couldn't seem to make the commitment. Now correct me here if I've misinterpreted something." A tear slid from her eye. "I told you I couldn't get the images of you and Ted out of my mind," she said in a wobbly voice. "I couldn't take it!" Hot tears flowed from her eyes. "What was I supposed to do? I ached for you night after night, wondering and then believing you and Ted were making love. It was killing me."

"You refused me."

"God, Sam, I only refused you because I didn't want only a part of you; I wanted all or nothing, dammit! I never once before asked any woman for a commitment. I waited for the special woman I knew would someday come. And that's you!" She wiped the tears from her cheeks. "I couldn't sleep with you, not knowing if and when you would leave me."

"But you should've known that I was playing a game with myself."

"How could I know that? I saw you and Ted together. It tortured me knowing that he was touching you as I had. I felt cheated, robbed."

"After you, J.C., no man could ever satisfy me. The night you saw me with Ted, nothing happened. I told you that. I couldn't respond to him. It was your touch I wanted and longed for."

"I didn't know, baby. I was so scared. I never felt this way about anyone before. You're in my blood, so much a part of me." She stroked Samantha's thigh. "I begged you our last night together to make a decision. I needed you that last time, but it only made me crave you more."

Samantha wiped her eyes with the back of her hand. "I came home tonight to tell you my decision. All the way home I couldn't think of anything except climbing into bed with you and feeling your body next to mine again, but you'd already given your love to another woman." Fresh tears flowed from her eyes. "Please go," she sobbed. "I need to think things through."

"No," J.C. whispered. "Never again." She caressed Samantha's skin as she wiped the tears from her face. "I'll never leave your bed again." She planted soft kisses on Samantha's neck. "Show me how much you want me, baby . . . how much you love me," she whispered.

"I do love you," Samantha said softly.

"Give me your heart, honey, like I've given you mine," J.C. said as her fingers explored the crevices of her lover.

A moan escaped from Samantha's throat. "You've always had my heart. I want to spend the rest of my life with you." She wrapped her legs around J.C.

"No more doubts?"

"No. Please love me, baby. Love me like you did our first time together."

J.C.'s lips met hers.

* * *

J.C. squeezed Samantha's hand as Jo rushed over to them. "How's Rachel?" J.C. asked.

Jo was beaming. "She's the one, J.C. I want you and Samantha to meet her very soon."

"I'm looking forward to it, Jo," J.C. answered, smiling. "I'm so happy for you."

Jo searched their faces. "And you two? Is everything all right?"

"It is now, Jo," Samantha answered. "You and I have a lot in common."

Jo looked at her quizzically.

"We almost lost the women we love."

Jo smiled. "I hope you and I can become friends, Samantha."

"I'd like that," Samantha answered.

"We'd better get inside," J.C. said.

"It's going to be okay, J.C.," Jo assured her as she patted her shoulder.

"Are you going to testify?"

She shrugged. "Ted said he wasn't sure."

J.C. took a deep breath, and then placed her hand on the door. "Just remember last night," Samantha whispered in her ear.

J.C. sat in the witness box, eyeing the spectators. She stole a glance at the jury, then looked to where Jo and Samantha were seated. The crowded courtroom filled her with fear. The outfit she was clad in added to her discomfort; she had never been at ease in a skirt, but Ted insisted that she wear one throughout the trial. Her toes felt pinched in her shoes.

She folded, then unfolded, her perspiring hands. Finally she placed them in her lap, hoping to mask her nervousness.

"Miss Markin, please tell the court your activities on the night of March 10."

She looked into Stuart Brewster's steel blue eyes, feeling the coldness emanating from them. It sent a chill up her spine. "I went to Harve's Bar for a few drinks, where I saw Samantha Wheeler, and we had a brief conversation." She looked at Samantha. Samantha's encouraging smile prompted her to continue. "The conversation wasn't friendly." She twisted her sweaty hands together. "I was angry, so I left the bar and walked to my apartment. Shortly afterward I fell asleep, but I woke up sometime in the middle of the night. I needed a drink," she said in a low voice.

"Please speak up, Miss Markin," Brewster's voice boomed.

"I said I needed a drink, but I couldn't find anything. I went to Sam's—Samantha Wheeler's apartment, and she gave me a drink. I wanted to spend the night, but she refused to let me. We got into an argument and she threw me out." She rapidly blinked her eyes.

"How did you get to Samantha Wheeler's apartment?"

She shrugged. "I don't remember."

He raised his eyes. "Continue, please."

"I left the apartment," she said in a quiet voice. "I don't remember anything after that. The next thing I do remember is waking up in jail." She looked up at him but felt only his cold, penetrating stare, as though he were looking into her very soul.

"What did you and Samantha Wheeler argue about?" the prosecutor asked.

"We argued about my drinking."

"You've stated that you are innocent in the murder of Harvey Barthow." Brewster paced back and forth in front of her for a few seconds. "How can you sit there and make such a claim when you just admitted to this court that you have no recollection of your actions for several hours?" he asked. "You cannot honestly say that you didn't commit this murder, Miss Markin, because you have no recollection of any of the events that transpired that night!"

J.C. jumped to her feet. "I didn't kill Harve!" she screamed. "I loved him . . . he was my friend! I am not a murderer!"

Judge Koviac slammed his mallet down as a deadly silence filled the room. "Order!" he demanded. "Counselor, please instruct your client as to the proper behavior in my courtroom! I will tolerate no further outbursts!"

Ted stood up, but before he had a chance to walk over to J.C., she had already seated herself.

"I apologize, Your Honor," she said.

"Continue," Judge Koviac said with a nod in Brewster's direction.

Brewster smiled smugly as he leaned over the railing, peering menacingly into her eyes. "You have a quick temper," he said.

J.C. ignored his taunt. Ted had warned her of this.

"Why did you go to Samantha Wheeler's apartment after you and she had argued earlier in the evening?" He tapped his finger in the palm of his hand.

"I . . . I knew that she would see me," J.C. slowly answered.

"How could you possibly know that?"

"Because in the past she always had. Whenever we argued, she would never refuse me if I needed anything." She took a deep breath. "We always made up."

"Did you go to her apartment primarily for sex?"

"Objection!" Ted roared. "That line of questioning has nothing to do with this case!"

"Objection sustained," Judge Koviac ordered.

Brewster frowned. "What do you do for a living?"

"I don't have a steady job."

"Surely you have living expenses. How do you support yourself?"

"Usually part time jobs see me through."

"I see. If you are found innocent, what would your future plans entail?"

"The most important thing is to improve my life. And I've already taken positive steps in that direction." She smiled confidently at him. "If this court finds me innocent, as I know I am, I intend to find a full time job and take some courses to further my education. I also would like to become active in the alcohol awareness program for teenagers."

"Do you blame your drinking for all of your problems?" he asked.

35-DRON

"No. No one forced me to drink. I'm responsible for my own actions while under the influence of alcohol."

"I see from your record that this isn't your first run-in with the law. Did your alcoholism contribute to those offenses?"

J.C. bit her bottom lip. "My life wasn't easy," she said in a shaky voice. "I drank to forget the pain, and sometimes it got me into trouble."

"Would you please elaborate for this court?"

"I was arrested once for getting into a fight, another for petit larceny, and the final time for possession of marijuana. These offenses were when I was a teenager. This is not the same as being accused of murder! I know that I didn't murder Harvey Barthow! He was the father I never had! I don't care what you believe!" she screamed. "Convict me for a crime I didn't commit! It'll be on your consciences!"

"Order!" Judge Koviac demanded again as the courtroom buzzed with voices. "I will not allow this type of conduct in my courtroom! This is your final warning, Miss Markin! You will refrain from any further outbursts or I will have you removed!"

Ted shot her a worried look, then angrily shook his head. He snapped his pencil in two.

Samantha and Jo glanced at one another. J.C. could see the fear etched on their faces. She was playing right into Brewster's hand. This is what he wanted the court to see; it would prove her uncontrollable behavior.

He glared into her eyes. She knew her own eyes flashed angrily at him. "Miss Markin, what proof do you have that you did not murder Harvey Barthow? You can't remember what you did that night after Samantha Wheeler asked you to leave. You have no recollection of being arrested outside of Harvey Barthow's apartment on the morning of March 11. Yet you still maintain your innocence and expect this court to believe you. At your first court appearance you stated that you had never left your apartment, then later you said you went to Samantha Wheeler's apartment. Why the discrepancy?" His voice was cold and demanding.

"You keep asking me the same questions over and over," she answered.

"And I'll continue to do so until I get some straight answers, Miss Markin!" he shouted, slamming his fist on the table.

J.C. inhaled deeply. "I lied because I thought if I said I had been to Samantha's, it would make me look guilty."

Brewster roared with laughter. "Please excuse me, Miss Markin, but your statement is ludicrous. I have no further questions, Your Honor."

"Your Honor, may I request permission to recall a witness to the stand?" Ted asked.

Judge Koviac peered at him through squinty eyes. "Very well."

"I'd like to recall Darcy Sebastion."

J.C. walked back to her seat, wondering what Ted was doing. She looked at Jo and Samantha and surmised from the expressions on their faces that they were wondering the same thing. She glumly sat down.

Darcy nervously walked slowly to the witness box, a noticible contrast to her self-assurance of the previous day.

"I'd like to remind you, Mrs. Sebastion, that you are still under oath," Judge Koviac stated.

"I understand," she replied as she seated herself.

J.C. watched Darcy worriedly eye the spectators. She looked like she was ready to vomit. Her face was ashen and her hands trembled. She caught J.C.'s eye, then quickly looked away.

"Mrs. Sebastion, would you please give an account of your activities on the night of March 10 and the early morning hours of March 11?" Ted asked.

Darcy looked up at him. "I went to Harve's Bar early in the evening. I saw J.C. and Samantha sitting together at the end of the bar. From the expressions on their faces, it appeared to me that they were involved in an intimate conversation."

"Mrs. Sebastion, I asked you what you were doing, not what Samantha Wheeler and Joyce Markin were doing," he impatiently interrupted.

35-DRON

"I'm sorry," she said in a low voice. "After a few minutes, I saw J.C. get up and storm out of the bar. I went to Samantha and tried to talk to her, but she was very cool toward me when I suggested that she bring J.C. up on assault charges for what J.C. had done to her the previous night. Since I wasn't getting through to Samantha, I decided to go home. I wasn't feeling well, so I retired early. The next morning I arose about 10:00 a.m. I turned on the radio and that's when I heard the news about Harvey Barthow. I quickly dressed and hurried over to Samantha's. I thought she might have some details."

Ted paced in front of the jury box, keeping his eyes glued on Darcy's face. She was becoming very uneasy. "Mrs. Sebastion, what if I told you that you were seen leaving Harvey Barthow's apartment fifteen minutes before Joyce Markin arrived? And what if I told you that you were seen approaching Joyce Markin outside of Samantha Wheeler's apartment in the early morning hours of March 11?" he asked, staring into her frightened eyes.

An eerie silence came over the courtroom as all eyes focused on Darcy, who nervously twisted the strap of her small purse.

"We're waiting for an answer, Mrs. Sebastion!"

Darcy let go of her purse and watched as it fell to the floor. She gripped the railing but didn't bother to retrieve her purse. "I—I . . ." She looked up. Her eyes darted back and forth to Ted, then to J.C.

"We're waiting, Mrs. Sebastion," Ted repeated in an icy tone.

Darcy gulped for air. "I . . . I followed J.C. to Samantha's apartment," she hoarsely whispered.

"Please speak up!" Ted demanded.

"I waited outside of Samantha's apartment building. I knew J.C. would come back out. She wouldn't stay long."

"How did you know that?"

"Samantha and J.C. had been arguing earlier. I knew that Samantha wouldn't talk to J.C. in J.C.'s drunken state."

"How did you know that J.C. would go over to Samantha Wheeler's apartment in the first place?"

"I waited night after night. It was only a matter of time before J.C. would go over there," she said disgustedly. "J.C. was obsessed with her."

"What happened when Joyce Markin left Samantha Wheeler's apartment?"

Darcy looked straight ahead.

J.C. noticed how Darcy's eyes had taken on a vacant glazed look. A cold chill swept over J.C. and she shivered even though it was warm and tight in the packed room.

"I told J.C. we had to go to Harve's apartment. I convinced her that Harve needed to see her immediately," Darcy answered. "I had to get her out of Samantha's life!" She looked pleadingly at Samantha. "It wasn't fair," she said in a broken voice.

"What wasn't fair?" Ted prodded.

"I tried to keep them apart. Samantha refused to end their relationship, so I had no choice! Can't you understand that?" Her eyes darted around the room from face to face as though she were looking for just one person to agree with her. "J.C. had what rightfully belonged to me!" she screeched.

"What happened when you arrived at Harvey Barthow's apartment, Mrs. Sebastion?" Ted asked.

She dabbed at her eyes with the tissues Ted handed her. "I . . . I told J.C. to wait in the car while I talked to Harve first." Her body shuddered. "When he answered his door I told him that I needed to talk to him about J.C. He immediately let me in and led me to his kitchen. I remember that he was drinking a cup of coffee and eating a sandwich. He asked me to join him, but I declined. He was concerned over J.C.'s well-being, and I assured him that she was okay, but I needed to discuss something with him."

"What happened then?"

Darcy briefly closed her eyes. "I saw the knife rack and walked over to it, pulling out a butcher knife. I think he assumed I was going to cut myself some cheese, because he pointed to the wedge of cheese on the table and joked about the size of the knife I had pulled out." Her voice grew quiet. "He kept looking at me, and it seemed like everything was going in slow motion. Then I walked toward him with the knife still clutched in my hand. His eyes widened; I think it must have been fear. I wonder if he knew what was going to happen. A horrible look came over his face, but before he could say another word, I plunged the knife into his chest. He just kept looking at me." She shuddered. "He opened his mouth and whispered 'J.C.' He wanted J.C.! I told him J.C. was the reason I was doing this! Blood trickled out of the corner of his mouth. But he kept whining for J.C." She started to laugh. "He wouldn't stop calling for her! I had to shut him up for good," she said bitterly. "I pulled the knife out and watched as his face contorted, and he gasped a few times. Then he slumped over. I had to make certain he was really dead so I stabbed him again. I couldn't stop myself. I pulled the knife out, then plunged it back in. I don't know how many times. There was blood everywhere." She glared at J.C. "He was still holding onto his sandwich, and the blood dripping from it almost made me vomit."

J.C.'s body heaved as sobs broke through her. Her anguished cries echoed throughout the room.

Ted wiped the sweat from his brow. "Mrs. Sebastion, what happened next?"

Darcy flashed him a bright smile, her confession seeming to make her believe that all was right now. "I left his apartment. I got into my car where J.C. was still waiting and told her to get out. She mumbled something about being tired and needing to go to sleep. I got back out of the car, opened the passenger side door, and pulled her out. She was clutching a bottle of whiskey. She wanted to know where we were going, so I told her I had to lock the car and to wait for me. She tried to get back in the car. She kept fighting me. I looked around and saw a brick, and I picked it up and hit her in the head with it." She laughed. "She rubbed her head, then started walking away from the car and toward the apartment building. I got in the car, then drove home."

"What did you do with your clothes?"

She smiled. "I took everything and burned it in the fireplace, then took a shower. I had blood splattered all over me and I couldn't stand it. When I was finished, I called the police, pretending that I was a neighbor. I reported hearing muffled sounds coming from Harvey's apartment and said that I was concerned for his safety." Her voice became clear and she looked straight ahead. "I was exhausted, so I went to bed. I'd never felt so tired." She was silent for a moment. When she spoke again, it was as though her personality had once again changed. "I thought she would finally get rid of J.C." She shook her head. "But, no, she wouldn't listen to reason." She looked at Ted with bewilderment. "Can you believe that she defended her?" Suddenly her eyes grew wild and she instantly was on her feet, running wildly to the defendant's table. She lurched at J.C., grabbing her shoulders before she was pulled away. "You don't deserve Samantha!" she screamed. "I should have killed you, not Harve!"

J.C. watched, frozen, as Darcy was handcuffed and led from the room screaming incoherently. She trembled as the realization that she was finally free overcame her.

Jo hugged her tightly. "It's over, honey. You're free."

J.C. smiled through her tears. "But Harve . . ."

Samantha stroked her hair. "Harve loved you, J.C. Just remember that. Harve saw his murderer."

"But why?" J.C. shook her head.

"She's sick," Jo said softly. "I thank God she didn't hurt you, too."

"But she did," J.C. whispered. "She killed Harve."

Jo looked at Samantha as she released her hold on J.C. "I think you and Samantha need to spend some time alone now."

"Thank you, Jo."

"Are you leaving?" J.C. asked.

"I'm going to spend some time with Rachel tonight. I have a lot of wasted time to make up to her. I'm going to go home and thank her for standing by me. I think I know what sacrificial love really means now." She smiled. "But don't worry, we'll still go to our meetings." She turned to Samantha. "Rachel wants to go to Al-Anon—it's for friends, spouses and families of alcoholics. The meetings are at the same time as ours. If you'd like to go please let me know?"

"Yes, thank you, Jo."

"Talk to you tomorrow," Jo said with a wink.

"How long is Ted going to be?" J.C. asked.

"It shouldn't be much longer," Samantha assured her. "Just think, honey, this is behind us now."

She shook her head. "It's still so strange. How did Ted know about Darcy? Did he say anything to you about a witness who saw her?"

"No, he didn't. I wonder how he came to suspect her in the first place."

"Well, she obviously made no secret to everyone of her feelings for you."

Samantha's eyes narrowed. "I've known Darcy all these years, and not once did she ever give me any inclination that she felt that way about me."

"What if she would have told you?" J.C. asked. "Do you think that you and she . . ."

"Don't even think it, J.C. The thought of being with her that way makes me sick to my stomach." She squeezed J.C.'s shoulder. "I'd never even thought about being with a woman until I met you."

J.C. cleared her throat. "At least I know why she hated me so much. It's funny, but in a way I can almost understand. I probably would have felt the same way." She grabbed Samantha's hand. "I was tortured thinking of you and Ted, but I wouldn't have killed someone because of it. Harve was an innocent victim." Her eyes filled with tears. "She killed him to punish me for being with you. If it weren't for Ted, I would be spending the rest of my life in prison. And the only thing I was ever guilty of was loving you."

"I know, honey, but now we have the rest of our lives to be together."

"It still bothers me that I was with Darcy that night and didn't even remember it."

"You're free from all that now. Please don't dwell on it. You're sober and starting over." She looked into J.C.'s eyes. "We're starting over."

"You're right."

Samantha hugged her tightly. "We can plan our future."

"I have so much to make up to you, " J.C. said softly.

Samantha shook her head.

"Yes." J.C. gazed into her eyes. "I want to make up for all the bad times. You stood by me through everything, and I treated you so cruelly."

"But I was as much at fault. I strung you along, not being able to make a decision. But do you understand why?" She searched J.C.'s face.

"Now I do."

"I have everything I've ever wanted. You."

* * *

"Well, Ted, I've got to hand it to you. You had me fooled." Brewster leaned close. "How did you know?"

"Darcy Sebastion told me," he answered.

Brewster gave him a puzzled look.

"She didn't come right out and tell me. It was what she didn't tell me," he explained, a wide grin encompassing his lean, tanned face. "I told you all along that I was working on a hunch."

"What if she wouldn't have confessed?"

"She had to. There was no way she could've kept her feelings for Samantha locked inside. I sensed those feelings the first time I talked to her. I just had to wait for the opportunity to crack her wide open."

He slapped Ted on the shoulder. "It's a good win, Ted. Go celebrate. You deserve it."

CHAPTER EIGHT

Ted leaned back into the sofa. "J.C., tell me your future plans."

She laughed. "I'm still dazed. After all these months of being frustrated, trying to prove my innocence, I still can't believe it's over and that I'm really free."

"Believe it," Samantha said. "Now you can accomplish all of those things you've wanted to."

J.C. smiled. "I don't know where to begin. Maybe I'll go to the community college next week and enroll in some classes."

"That's a good idea," Ted said. "What are you interested in?"

She shrugged, then laughed again. "I don't know, maybe computers."

"Sounds interesting. I'm sure something will catch your interest." He patted her hand. "You'll still continue AA?"

"Definitely. I'm going to get more involved. Jo and I will go to AA, and Samantha and Jo's girlfriend Rachel are going to go to Al-Anon."

"That's super."

"Can I ask you something, Ted?" Her voice grew serious.

"Anything, J.C."

"What's going to happen to Darcy?"

He frowned. "She will undergo a thorough psychiatric evaluation. In her present state of mind, though, I imagine she'll be institutionalized for quite some time. If she's ever determined to be sane, then she will serve a life term in prison." He eyed J.C. thoughtfully. "What was the first thing that went through your mind when she admitted her guilt?"

She let her breath out quickly. "I don't know . . . shock, especially finding out how she felt about Samantha. I couldn't believe that she was so obsessed with her love for Samantha that she would commit murder." Her eyes narrowed. "It must have ripped her apart inside, knowing that her money could buy her everything but Samantha. I had the one thing she wanted. And she couldn't tell Samantha."

"I wonder why she never hinted it to me?" Samantha mused.

"How could she, Sam?" J.C. asked. "If you weren't interested, then it could have destroyed your friendship. At least this way, she still got to keep at least a part of you in her life."

"That makes sense, J.C.," Ted agreed.

"I can speak from experience, because when Samantha and I weren't together, it was the worst thing I ever had to go through. It was horrible thinking I would never have her in my life in any way again."

"But you never have to worry about that again," Samantha said with a smile.

J.C. kissed her cheek. "Well, if you two don't mind, I'd like to take a shower."

"Go ahead," Samantha replied.

After J.C. was out of the room, Samantha turned to Ted. "I never want to see her hurt again."

"I'll probably never completely understand what you and J.C. share, Samantha, but I know that it's something everyone longs for and wishes he or she had."

* * *

J.C.'s hand trembled as she dialed the number the operator had given her. This was something she knew she had to do. She had given it much thought, but still she worried. She needed to put closure on her past—all of it. She hadn't mentioned to Jo or Samantha what she had planned to do. This had to be her own decision. No matter the outcome of the impending conversation, she would know that she, at least, had tried to make amends and put the upleasant past to rest.

"Hello," an impatient voice said, indicating that her time was too valuable to waste.

"Jody, this is J.C.," she said nervously.

There was a long silence, making J.C. think the line had been disconnected, when Jody's voice came back over the line. "It's been a long time. If you want money, forget it!"

"No, no, Jody, I don't want any money. I need to talk to you. Would it be possible for us to get together?"

"We have nothing to say to one another, J.C. The past is dead," she said coldly. "I did hear, though, that you've gotten yourself into some very serious trouble. Murder?"

"No, the trial is over and I was found innocent. I was framed."

"Looks like you lucked out again. I haven't had a chance to read the papers all week."

"Jody, there are some things that need to be said face to face, not over the telephone."

"What good would it do, J.C.? There is nothing left for us to say to one another. When the children died, my feelings for you died, too."

"Jody, please! I'm not trying to hurt you. Neither of us has truly healed from their deaths. I need to talk to you. Then we'll be able to get on with our lives. Please?" she pleaded.

"I don't know, J.C.," she hesitated. "I don't think it's a good idea."

"Please, Jody. You'll never hear from me again, then. I promise you. I need to see you. I've been haunted all these years. Just let me have some closure."

She hesitated. "All right. I'll see if I can get a flight out next weekend. Call me in a few days."

"Thank you, Jody," J.C. gratefully whispered. She set the phone down, then walked to the patio door. "Okay, you two break it up!" she teased, strolling out onto the patio.

Samantha grabbed her hand. "Come sit with us."

"I need to tell you something, Samantha," she said.

"Would you like me to leave?" Ted asked.

"Oh, no," J.C. quickly assured him.

"What is it?" Samantha questioned.

"I called Jody."

Samantha raised her eyebrows. "Why?"she asked uneasily.

"I need to put things right between us." She saw the anxious look in Samantha's eyes. "I need to put that part of my life to rest. She and I never talked after the accident. I think she always thought that I never cared about the kids' deaths. She needs to know how much they meant to me. She also needs to know that I've finally straightened out my life."

"Are you going there?"

"No, she's flying out next weekend." Her eyes pleaded with Samantha's for understanding. "Is it okay?"

"Of course." She pulled J.C. down next to her. "I'll agree to anything that'll make you feel better, J.C. Besides, I wouldn't want you to think that I'm a jealous, insecure woman," she teased.

J.C. laughed.

"I do have one question, though."

J.C. raised her eyebrows.

"Why did you wait so long to tell me about Jody?"

J.C. shrugged. "I couldn't when we first met. And then we had so many problems. I decided that the less you knew about my past relationships, the better off I would be. Besides, the time was never right. I don't know . . . maybe I was trying to run away from that part of my life, too. I think somewhere inside I almost convinced myself that it never did happen. I was trying to make the hurting go away."

Samantha put an arm around her, drawing her close.

"But the pain never did disappear. It was always with me. Even drinking wouldn't erase it. Sometimes it hurt so bad I even thought of suicide." Tears glistened in her eyes. "When I met you, Sam, I knew I had something to live for. You really cared about me, and I would've done anything for you, but I couldn't stop drinking because everything would be too real again. All the bad things would seep back into my mind and soul."

"I never meant to add to your pain, J.C. But I know my indecisiveness hurt you deeply."

She took a deep breath. "There were times when I felt like you were ashamed to have me around or have your friends and associates meet me. You never wanted me at your social events. I was good enough to be your lover, but not your friend."

"That's how Jody treated you, too?"

She nodded.

"J.C., I was so wrong. I shouldn't have cared what anyone else thought. I should have put you first."

"Before I moved in with you, you would invite me to dinner, then call a few minutes before I was to come over to tell me that something had come up. When I did move in, you would ask me to leave for a few hours so you could entertain. Later I would find out that Darcy was one of the guests."

"I knew that you and she didn't care for one another. I was so busy trying to make everyone else happy that I didn't see what it was doing to you."

"Well, that's all behind us now," she said with a smile. She got up and walked over to the railing, placing her hands on it as she gazed down at the city lights and drinking in the breathtaking view. "Life is so strange. Just when you think you have everything figured out, something else comes along to screw up your mind." She turned around to face both of them. "I'm not too great with words," she apologized as her face turned crimson, "but I don't know how I would have survived these past months without the both of you believing in me."

Samantha's eyes brimmed with tears as she walked over to J.C. "I never want to think of you not being with me. Let's change the subject before I start crying."

J.C. put an arm around her waist. "I know I still have some work to do on my temper and my jealousy." She laughed. "I remember how much I despised you the minute I laid eyes on you, Ted. I refused to believe that you truly wanted to help me. That's what I thought about you, too, Sam. I thought I was just a new toy and you would toss me out when you'd had enough of me. You two came from worlds that were strange to me." She stroked Samantha's arm. "I abused your love because I was afraid I was losing you. I wanted you to want me as much as I wanted you."

"I never should've put you through that, J.C. It wasn't fair to you. In your place, I would have felt the same way."

"It's too lonely in this big world without someone to love you by your side," J.C. answered. "Now we need to find the perfect woman for Ted," she laughed. "But I have a slight problem in that area."

"Why's that?" he asked with a laugh in his voice.

"All my friends are lesbians."

* * *

J.C. paced back and forth. "I don't know what to say to Jody. I had it all planned out in my mind, but now I can't even think clearly," she whined. "Do I look all right?"

Samantha threw her head back and laughed. "You look beautiful. Will you stop pacing? You're going to wear a hole in the carpet."

Waves of emotion pulsated through her. J.C. was stunning. Her dark eyes glowed and her long, loosely worn hair magnified the whiteness of the outfit she was wearing. J.C. gripped the cross hanging from her neck.

"Did you talk to Jo?" Samantha asked.

"Yes, but she said I'll survive. Some help she was."

Samantha tried to hide her amusement. "Jo's right."

"I know."

It suddenly occurred to Samantha that J.C.'s nervousness was like that of a teenager waiting for her date to pick her up for the prom. She became uneasy. J.C. was seeing her former lover; a woman she had shared time with. What if old sparks rekindled?

J.C. stopped pacing, perhaps picking up on Samantha's uneasiness. She walked over to her, then tilted her head until their eyes met. "You're the one I want to spend the rest of my life with." She tenderly kissed her lips.

The doorbell rang. "I'll get it," Samantha said, leaving J.C. to compose herself.

J.C. glumly stared out of the window at the hustling city below. She took a deep breath, exhaled, and repeated the process. Seconds later she heard voices behind her. She had to turn around, but she couldn't bring herself to do so. Not yet. She felt a warm hand on her shoulder, and a tremor went through her.

"I'll be out on the patio, J.C. Why don't you and Jody use the library?" She affectionately gave J.C.'s shoulder a squeeze before removing her hand.

J.C. heard her leave the room but still couldn't bring herself to face her former lover. Echoes of the past flooded her senses. A child's bubbly laughter from the street below brought a rush of tears to her eyes and, for a brief moment, she was transported back to a place in time that was unbearable to her.

"Are you going to stare out of the window all day, or do you want to talk to me? I have a tight schedule and had to break several appointments to be here. God only knows why I came in the first place." The voice was sharp and demanding. It was the voice that J.C. remembered so very well, the voice that had sometimes made J.C. feel that she was the child and Jody the mother, instead of lovers, in their turbulent relationship.

J.C. whirled around, looking Jody squarely in the eye. Jody was the same obnoxious, self-centered woman she had always been. Time hadn't seemed to mellow her. "It's good to see you, Jody," she said, trying to make her voice sound pleasant and at the same time trying to control the anger she felt surfacing within her chest. "Let's go into the library."

Jody followed her through the spacious apartment, commenting on Samantha's fine taste in furnishings. When they reached the library she abruptly halted, marveling at the elaborate display of books on the shelves. "These are worth a fortune!" she exclaimed. "How in the world did someone like you get involved with the Wheelers?"

Her arrogance annoyed J.C. "The same way I got involved with you," she answered calmly.

Jody whirled around, amusement on her face. "I see."

"Samantha has had a stabilizing effect on my life," she said. She ushered her to a large leather chair. "Can I get you a drink?"

"Will you join me?"

J.C. emphatically shook her head. "I've been sober for over a year now," she proudly boasted.

"And you're not tempted to join me?"

"No, I'm not."

She looked at her suspiciously. "I don't believe you, but yes, I'd like a drink . . . scotch and water, please."

She watched her fix the drink. "You've lost weight."

"Yes, some." J.C.'s hand trembled slightly as she handed her the drink.

Jody waited until J.C. poured herself some cola over ice, then watched her carry the drink in an unsteady hand and seat herself directly across from her. J.C. became nervous as Jody's icy blue eyes bore through her. Jody leaned back comfortably in her chair, taking caution not to wrinkle her designer dress. "Let's stop playing games, J.C., I'm here. Now get to the point of this meeting."

"I want you to know that I have no bitter feelings toward you, Jody."

She grimaced. "You have no bitter feelings toward me?" Her voice was hostile. "Why should you?"

"Please, Jody, just listen to what I have to say. Please humor me."

She rolled her eyes. "Go ahead," she said sharply.

She took a deep breath. "I've thought about our relationship a lot over the past few years, but mostly this past year when I became sober. I know that we never stood a chance. We were doomed from day one and there was no way we could've ever survived. We were total opposites. I tried to be the person you wanted me to be, but I couldn't." She frowned. "I used to think that you were trying to recapture your youth with me. You knew about my excessive drinking and partying when you met me. You can't deny that. You opened up a world to me that I had only seen in movies or read about in books. I was overwhelmed! We had many good times in the beginning, though, and I'll always treasure those memories. But then you changed. You kept climbing the corporate ladder, leaving me to struggle on the first rung. I reached my hand out to you, but you never looked down, only continued to climb. I was frightened and lonely. Alcohol was the only comfort I had. It helped me through the long, cold nights while you were out socializing. I needed you, but you turned your back on me. I couldn't count on you anymore. You'll never know how many nights I cried myself to sleep because I didn't know how to reach you. With every passing day we were drifting further and further apart, and I knew that I had to leave if I were ever to survive." She lowered her eyes, watching the ice melting in her glass.

Jody took a deep breath but said nothing.

"I tried to please you and satisfy all of your needs. But in time I realized that I was just a nanny to your children and a playmate for you." She looked into Jody's emotionless eyes. "I loved you. I couldn't stand to live in your world anymore, so I had to escape into a world of my own where I could find protection from the pain. I couldn't feel your love anymore. There was nothing to hold on to. If I didn't leave you, I was afraid that I would lose my mind. I had no plans; I just needed to get away from you." Tears streamed from her eyes, and she grabbed a tissue.

"All these years," she continued, "I've relived the night of the accident over and over. I know I was to blame. Their deaths should have made me stop drinking, but it didn't. I was so sick inside that it made me drink more. I tried to block that night out of my mind. My attitude toward life changed—I didn't give a damn about anything anymore. After I was released from the hospital, I didn't have any money or anywhere to go. I picked up women in bars just to have a place to sleep for the night. Then I went back to Harve. In time I confessed to Jo—you remember her—what had happened. We moved in together, but it didn't work out. We were different people. We still loved each other, but we were too much alike. We were two alcoholics trying to make a life together."

Jody stared intently at her, but still kept her silence.

"Then one night everything changed. Just like that. I met Samantha. I didn't feel alone anymore. I had a friend. I had someone who loved me. We took care of each other. But we had our share of problems due to my drinking." She took a long swallow from her glass. "We separated, and I was alone and vulnerable once again. The only friend I had left was Harve. I didn't even turn to Jo. I knew Harve understood. He was always there for me. His death and my indictment brought Samantha and me back together, and it was then that I came clean to her about you and the kids. I know I can't change the past, but I did change what my future with alcohol had in store for me. I want to have a positive effect on people. I know that saying I'm sorry for the pain and suffering I've caused you isn't enough, but I am sincere."

Jody gazed at her for a few seconds. "I can see that you are trying to deal with life realistically now, J.C." She finished her drink. "But I don't know if I'll ever be able to find forgiveness in my heart for you. My children are dead because of you. I still wish that you would have died instead of them." Her voice was bitter. "You destroy everything you touch. I loved you and gave you everything, but it was never enough! Did you ever realize how I felt? I was trying to hold onto someone half my age. I saw how you looked at girls on the street. I tried to stay young for you, but I couldn't compete. You walked out on me and I had nothing left. I was wrong to use my children to try to hold on to you!"

"Our age difference never mattered to me," J.C. said in a low voice.

Jody ignored her. "When I received the phone call telling me about the accident, I rushed to the hospital, but the children were already dead." Her voice cracked, then broke. "I couldn't bear to be near you. Everything I felt for you died with them."

J.C. walked over to her and put her arms around her.

"Please don't," Jody sniffed.

"No, say what you need to say to me, Jody. Tell me all those things you wanted to say to me but never did. That's the only way you'll heal."

Jody swallowed hard. "It took all of my willpower not to go to the hospital to see you in the following weeks. I still couldn't get you out of my system. I thought I had, but remembrances of you popped up everywhere. But if I saw you, I felt like I would be betraying my children. I know that it doesn't make sense, but that was how I felt."

"I want you to be happy, Jody. You deserve to be."

She jumped to her feet. "I need to get out of here. I don't need to stir up old hurts."

"Jody, please don't go," J.C. pleaded, grabbing her arm.

"Please don't touch me."

"Listen to me, for God's sake!"

Jody turned around.

"Maybe if we both try, we can sit down like two mature adults and help each other through this pain."

"Why does it matter anymore? We have separate lives now."

"I think we need to do it for the kids." Her eyes implored her. "For their memory."

"They loved you so much, J.C."

"You can never doubt my love for them."

"I never did." She sighed tiredly.

"Are you all right, Jody?'

"I think I will be." She smiled faintly. "What are your plans now that the trial is behind you?"

"I'm going to take some classes at night and work in one of Samantha's companies during the day."

She raised her eyebrows. "Entry level?"

She nodded. "I want to work my way up like everyone else has had to."

"Good for you." She studied her carefully. "You're happy, aren't you?"

"Yes, Jody, I am."

"Samantha is good for you."

"That she is. Do you have someone?" she asked.

"Yes. We've been together for three years. She's a financial consultant . . . that's how I met her."

"Good."

"She didn't want me to come here today. It's not jealousy; she just didn't want the dredging up of the past to hurt me."

"She sounds like a very considerate woman."

"She is. I'm happy, J.C. She fulfills me."

J.C. smiled. "I'm glad for you." She toyed with her necklace. "Jody, maybe someday you'll find it in your heart to forgive me." Her voice was soft.

"I don't know. I can't yet."

She extended her hand. "At least maybe now we can be friends."

Jody smiled awkwardly. "You have a way with people, J.C." She took her hand. "Goodbye."

After she saw Jody out, J.C. silently watched Samantha, her heart full with the happiness life had finally given her.

Samantha looked up from her magazine. "How'd it go?" she asked with a bright smile.

J.C. sat down in a lounge chair and kicked off her sandals. "The things I wanted to say to her didn't seem to come out right. I put her on the defensive. But we parted no longer enemies." Her voice echoed the frustration within her.

"Did you want something more out of this meeting?"

"I need to hold you."

Samantha walked over to her and knelt beside the chair. J.C. gently stroked her head.

"Maybe you expected a forgiveness she's not ready to give, honey. I thought she was very polite, attractive, and charming. What more did you want?"

J.C. exhaled loudly . "It's just me. I don't know what I wanted. Maybe for her to pat me on the back and tell me what a good girl I am because I've stopped drinking and screwing up everyone's lives!"

Samantha grabbed her hand, gently enclosing it in her own. "I could've been very jealous, J.C. It's hard for me knowing you've been with other women. You shared something very special with Jody."

"You never need to worry, baby," she whispered. "No other woman could ever compare with you. I love you so much that sometimes it scares the hell out of me."

"Why?" she asked, raising her eyebrows.

"I have this fear that someday you'll meet someone who will be better for you. Someone who can fulfill the needs that I'm incapable of filling."

She tossed her head back and laughed. "No chance of that. You're my first and last. I was your virgin," she teased. J.C. grinned. "Maybe we need to quit being insecure and concentrate on the wonderful future lying ahead of us."

"I agree." She ran the back of her hand over Samantha's soft cheek. "I've got to get ready for the meeting tonight."

"What time are Jo and Rachel coming over?"

"About seven," J.C. answered.

"Thank you for letting me share this part of your life with you, J.C." She held her close.

"You don't know what it means to me to have you in the next room, knowing you're there for me."

She brushed her lips softly against J.C.'s. "I want to share in everything that affects you."

CHAPTER NINE

"J.C., can I talk to you after the meeting?" Christy asked.

"Sure," J.C. replied, taking her seat next to Jo.

"Do you want me to hang around?" Jo asked.

J.C. shook her head. "Nah, I'll have Christy give me a ride home when we've finished. Will you take Samantha home?"

"Of course, silly. We brought her, didn't we?" She laughed. "She and Rachel have really hit it off."

"You seem different, Jo," J.C. said quietly

Jo frowned. "I don't think so."

"Yeah, you are," she teased. "More relaxed."

She grinned. "I don't know why I was so afraid of a commitment . . . it's the best thing that ever happened to me."

"I knew the love bug would bite one of these days."

Jo laughed. "I learned so much from what you were going through with Samantha. That's what I was putting Rachel through."

"Well, we've got two great women."

"You've got that right." She turned to J.C., her voice growing serious. "We're extremely lucky, J.C."

"That we are," she agreed. "They could be jealous of our past together, but they're both so understanding."

She nodded. "We have so much to be grateful for."

J.C. squeezed her hand.

After the meeting Jo and J.C. watched the group from Al-Anon drift into the room. Samantha and Rachel hurried over to them, quickly followed by Christy. "I need to talk to J.C., Samantha, if it's all right with you?" Christy asked.

"Of course." Samantha smiled warmly. "You'll give her a ride home?"

"Certainly. Don't worry, she'll be fine."

"She's like a mother hen sometimes," J.C. teased.

"Someone's got to keep you in line," Samantha returned the playful badgering. She kissed J.C.'s cheek. "I'll see you later."

"So, what's up?" J.C. asked brightly.

"Let me round up Mark. We've got a surprise for you."

Ten minutes later they were seated around a small table in the back of a diner, sipping from large mugs of coffee.

Mark set his cup down. "It's almost your second year anniversary, J.C."

She smiled proudly. "I never thought I'd make it."

"But you did," Christy beamed.

"So, what did you need to talk to me about?"

"Do you remember when you told me and Mark that you wanted to talk to teenagers about alcohol abuse?"

She nodded.

Mark was grinning. "Christy and I feel that you're ready."

A smile broke over J.C.'s face. "That's been my dream."

"It gets even better," Christy added. J.C. looked at her quizzically.

"The high school on the south side has decided to have someone available to counsel the kids. They wanted someone who would really understand them and be on their level, someone who's been there. It's important to have someone they can trust."

"Are you serious?" she asked excitedly.

"It'll be for a couple of hours a day. We'll be available for the stickier situations." Mark patted her shoulder. "Do you want to do it?"

"Yes," she beamed. "When do I start?"

"We've got to iron out a few details, but it should be within a month."

"Wait till Samantha and Jo hear," she said ecstatically.

J.C. couldn't wait to share her news with Samantha, but first she needed time alone to reflect on all the goodness happening at long last in her life. She kicked off her shoes, enjoying the feel of the carpet beneath her bare feet, then removed her clothes and walked naked through the apartment, enjoying the peacefulness. She entered the master bedroom, grabbed a nightgown, and pulled on a pair of slippers. She padded to the patio door and opened it wide. The city lay before her in all its nighttime wonder. She felt so alive. She breathed deeply, gazing ahead at the bright city. She felt like a queen looking down on her kingdom. The world was hers. Life surged through her veins, grateful at long last to escape the suppression that had encumbered her for so long. The shell was broken and she was emerging into a new life, fresh and full of wonder at what lay ahead of her. She walked out onto the patio, then over to the railing. She gulped deep breaths of the cool night air, breathing life into herself.

After thirty minutes she walked back into the apartment. She removed her nightgown and slippers, then climbed between the cool sheets. She gently kissed Samantha's cheek, nestling close to her, letting the sounds of Samantha's slumber lull her into a deep, restful sleep.

She stirred, hours later, when she felt Samantha's warm hand on her thigh. She moaned softly as the lips she loved pressed against hers. Her arms went around Samantha, drawing her close.

"I've got to go on a business trip for a few days, honey," Samantha whispered between kisses.

J.C. kissed her neck. "I don't know if I can stand to be apart from you. This bed will feel so empty and lonely."

Samantha grabbed her hands. "I know, but it'll only be for a few days. When I come home, we'll celebrate. Anything you want to do."

"There's only one thing I want to do," she whispered, pulling her down on top of herself.

* * *

"Are you certain you'll be all right?' Samantha asked. "I'm sure Jo and Rachel would love to have you stay with them until I return."

She laughed. "I'll be fine. I'll be seeing them every night to go to meetings."

"Please be careful, J.C."

"I will," she promised. "I'll be busy with work and getting ready for the counseling."

Samantha frowned. "I don't approve of you working in the factory."

J.C. placed a finger to Samantha's lips to silence her. "We've been all through that. I want to start at the bottom. I want to be treated like anyone else in production; no favors."

She sighed, knowing J.C. was adamant. "Okay. Whatever makes you happy."

She grinned. "You make me happy. Now get going. Your taxi's been waiting for ten minutes." She embraced her, holding her tightly before releasing her. "I've got to get ready for work."

* * *

"J.C., there's someone who insists on seeing you. He wouldn't give his name. He said he wouldn't leave until he talks to you. Should I call security?" Karla, the pretty young receptionist, yelled above the roar of the machines.

"He wouldn't give his name?" she asked impatiently.

"No," Karla said.

"All right. Tell him I'll be with him in a few minutes," she said, grabbing a soiled rag hanging loosely from her back pocket. She quickly wiped her oily hands on it, then rammed it back into her pocket. She was cranky and tired. Sleeping had been difficult without the security of Samantha next to her last night. She walked to the main office. She felt out of place in her denim one-piece work suit as she observed the well-manicured and immaculately dressed office workers.

“I left him in the conference room, J.C.,” Karla said, escorting her to the room.

“Thank you, Karla.”

J.C. slowly opened the door, wondering who was behind it. Once inside the room, she stared in disbelief at her visitor. “What do you want?” she asked harshly.

“Now, that’s no way to greet your big brother, Sis,” the man replied, watching her every move from his perch on top of the conference table.

“What do you want?” she asked again.

“I just thought it might be nice to have a little family reunion. How many years has it been now?” He leered at her, showing off yellow-stained teeth.

“”Not enough as far as I’m concerned. Look, Johnny, I have nothing to say to you, or anyone else in the family, for that matter. You can all just stay the hell out of my life!”

“Little Miss High and Mighty! I lose track of you for ten years and what happens? I pick up a newspaper and see your picture on the front page. The Markins always aspired for the top! It almost blew my mind! Murder! I had all kinds of bets out that you did it, but you let me down,” he scoffed. “The papers say you’ve reformed. I got a kick out of that one. You, reform? Not my little sister, I said. She loves the fast life too much.” He smirked at her. “I want to know your secret to success, Sis. You’re in the big leagues now. A close personal friend of Samantha Wheeler’s. You of all people,” he laughed again. “What does a rich bitch like her see in you?” he asked sarcastically. “But that’s right. How could I forget? You two are lovers. When I read that, I almost puked!”

“Shut up,” J.C. demanded. “You don’t know Samantha, and I certainly don’t care what you think about me. As though your opinion would ever count for anything.”

“Are all those high society bitches perverts? I’ll bet they are. She’s probably only using you to play out her fantasies,”

5-DRON

he taunted. "You must be feeling pretty lonely at night since she's away on business."

"How do you know that?"

"I called to speak with her, stupid."

"Why?"

He laughed. "Let's just say that it's private—something between me and her."

"Don't you ever do anything to her or . . ."

"Or what?" Anger came into his eyes. "When's your lover coming back? Maybe she's found a new playmate," he goaded her.

"Get out of here, you bastard!"

"Not until you do your big brother a favor." He eyed her warily. "I need some cash. I've got to have it today," he insisted.

J.C. looked with repugnance at her brother's filthy clothes and matted black hair. "I wouldn't give you a dime," she spat.

He leaped off the table and grabbed her by the collar of her shirt. "Maybe you didn't hear me, Sis. I'm not asking you, I'm telling you. I want five thousand bucks! That's pocket money to your rich lover. I'm not playing games here!"

His hot, stinking breath repulsed her. She turned her nostrils away from his mouth. "What's the money for?"

"None of your fucking business!" He tightened his hold on her.

"Get your filthy hands off me," she shouted. "If you're not out of here in exactly five seconds, I'm calling security!"

He forcefully released her, sending her reeling backward against the wall. "I'll see you later," he threatened, pointing a long, skinny finger under her nose.

"Asshole," she muttered as he slammed the door behind himself. She bit her bottom lip. Her past, everything she wanted to forget, now seemed to be coming back to haunt her, to let her know who and what she truly was. She wished she could escape, but there was none. Before, losing herself in alcohol had seemed the only way out, but not now. She was stronger; she would overcome this, too. She had gotten through all the other obstacles and she could survive this.

* * *

After Jo and Rachel saw her safely inside, J.C. luxuriated in a bath, savoring the warm water that soothed her tired, aching bones. Today had left her physically drained. Five machines broke down, and she and her assistant had had to repair them before the end of the shift. She yawned. She got out of the tub and toweled herself dry. She slipped into a pair of silk pajamas Samantha had given her on her last birthday, then fixed a sandwich and settled down in front of the TV. She found a favorite old movie and lost herself in it for the next two hours.

After the movie ended she turned off the TV, then picked up the phone and dialed Samantha's hotel. When she received no answer, she dejectedly carried her dishes to the kitchen and placed them in the sink.

The ringing of the doorbell startled her. She couldn't figure who would be calling at this late hour, and why John hadn't rung that she had a visitor. He personally knew the only people allowed up without notification.

She tiptoed to the door and peered through the peephole. She could see no one, so turned to leave when the bell rang again. She looked again through the peephole but saw no one there. *Probably a loose wire*, she thought. An uneasy feeling came over her, but she shook it off, attributing it to being overtired. She yawned, then headed for the bedroom. The bell sounded again.

"Dammit," she muttered as she headed once again to the door. "Who's there?"

She heard nothing, and still saw no one through the peephole. "I know someone's out there!" she shouted.

A loud thump outside the door startled her. She flung the door wide open. A brown paper bag lay on the floor. "What the hell?" she said, bending down to pick it up. The sack contained a bottle.

"I told you I'd return," her brother said, coming out of the shadows.

She was frightened but didn't want him to see it. If she did, that would give him the edge.

Before she could say anything, though, he clamped a hand tightly over her mouth and shoved her inside the apartment. He kicked the door shut with his boot-clad foot, then released his hold on her. "I came for the money," he hissed.

"I don't have any money," she shouted. "Now get the hell out of here before I call the police!"

"Do you really think I'm going to let you call the cops?" he asked, ripping the cord from the phone. "I'll give you one minute to hand over the money," he snarled as he picked up an antique vase. "It sure would be a shame if these pretty vases here got busted—accidentally, I mean." His dark eyes flashed wildly. "I don't have much time. Give it to me. Now!"

"You make me sick!" She spit at him, taking him by surprise. He momentarily loosened his grip on her. She ran towards the kitchen, but he was too quick for her. He grabbed her arm.

"This is your last chance," he threatened. "Give me the money!"

"You can rot in the gutter first!" she screamed.

He brought the back of his hand up and slapped her in the mouth. She tasted blood. "You filthy pig!" she screamed, kicking at him. He grabbed her leg, sending her crashing to the floor. He raised his fists, then sent them pummeling into her face.

* * *

Jenny stood outside the apartment door, fumbling in her coat pocket for the key. Once the door was unlocked she grabbed her cleaning bag, then walked into the apartment. She set her gear in the entrance hall, then turned on the lights, humming softly as she made her way into the living room. She stopped when she saw the overturned furniture and smashed glass. She hurried to the telephone to call the police and glanced at her wristwatch. It must have happened within the hour right after J.C. left for work. Someone must have been watching, waiting for her to leave, she surmised.

She quickly dialed 911. "I need to report a robbery," she shrieked as her eye caught sight of something next to the kitchen door.

"What is your name?" the dispatcher asked.

"Oh my God!" Jenny screamed, moving closer to the door. "Please get an ambulance!" she shouted, dropping the phone. She knelt down to where J.C. lay crumpled in a heap.

"No . . . no . . . no," she moaned observing the dried blood splotched on J.C.'s face and body. Her eyelids were swollen, and her arm lay in a twisted position behind her. The pajamas she had worn were now nothing but threads clinging to her battered body. "J.C.," she called over and over. "You're going to be okay," she whispered, picking up the limp hand. "Dammit! Where is the ambulance?" she frantically asked aloud. She couldn't feel a pulse. "Come on, J.C., wake up!" she pleaded.

Fear swept through her as she tried in vain to revive J.C. Time was a blur, and she didn't hear the attendant until he was next to her, gently pulling her away from J.C. "Thank God, you're here," she choked.

The attendant quickly grabbed his equipment. "Jay, get the stretcher over here. She's got to get to the hospital!" he ordered. "I can't stabalize her."

Jenny watched, blurry-eyed, as different apparatus were attached to J.C.

"I'm getting a faint reading! Let's go!" he insisted.

A police officer took Jenny's elbow. "I'm Officer Donovan. I'm going to need to ask you a few questions."

She looked into his kind eyes. "I can't believe this happened. Not to J.C. and Samantha," she cried.

"This is J.C. Markin? The woman acquitted of the Barthow homicide?"

"Yes," she nodded rapidly. "Is she going to be okay?" Her voice quivered.

"I can't say," he said softly. "You found her?"

"Yes."

5-DRON

His gaze swept the room. "This happened sometime during the night. She obviously surprised the burglar during the robbery. It looks like she put up a fight."

He looked at the pictures that had been torn from the wall, and the fragments of what had been Samantha's antique vase collection. Several pieces of furniture were overturned or broken beyond repair. He watched as J.C. was loaded onto the stretcher. "Can you give me your full name?"

"Jenny Wilkins."

"What is your relationship to Miss Markin?"

"I'm employed by Samantha Wheeler as a housekeeper. I come in twice a week."

"How long have you worked for her?"

"Almost seven years," she replied.

"Can you tell me what, if anything, out of the ordinary you may have observed upon your arrival this morning?" He stared purposefully at her.

"I let myself in as I always do. I assumed J.C. had gone to work."

"What about Samantha Wheeler?"

"She's out of town on a business trip."

"Do you have much contact with either of them?"

She shook her head. "Very rarely. But on the occasion I do see them, they are very nice women." A thought suddenly came to Jenny. "Do you think this is related to J.C.'s acquittal?"

He became pensive. "That's an area I'm certain will be explored. That'll be all for now, Miss Wilkins. We'll be in touch if there's anything further."

She helplessly looked around herself.

The officer radioed the station. Minutes later, the apartment was being dusted for fingerprints and swept for anything which could aid them in their efforts to find the perpetrator.

Officer Donovan walked over to the head detective on the case. "Brad, have you come up with anything?"

The detective wearily shook his head. "Not yet. We have some blood samples. Maybe she clawed him. We won't know too much until she comes to."

"If she does," Donovan replied. "Dammit, I pray she does."

* * *

"Jo, she's so pale," Samantha cried as she looked at J.C.'s bruised and swollen face. "What kind of bastard would do this to her?"

Jo drew her into her arms. She blinked hard, then let her own tears fall. "I don't know. I blame myself. I should've insisted that she stay with Rachel and me."

"It's not your fault," Samantha whispered.

Rachel patted Jo's back. "None of us had any inkling that something like this would ever happen."

"She's been through so much," Samantha cried as her heart broke. She desperately yearned to cradle J.C. in her arms. "I can't stand this! Why aren't the police doing anything?"

"They're doing all they can," Rachel said, trying to soothe her.

Ted hurried into the room. "Any change?"

"No. They don't know if she's even going to live," Samantha said in a cracked voice.

"Why don't we all go down to the cafeteria for some coffee? You girls look like you could use some."

"I don't want any, Ted." She nodded to Rachel and Jo. "You two go. I want to be with J.C."

Jo grabbed Rachel's arm. "Let's leave them alone for awhile."

Ted softly laid a hand on her shoulder. "You've been here for over twenty-four hours, Samantha. You've got to have some rest. We're not sure when she'll come out of it."

Samantha's eyes grew wide. "I want to be here when she does."

He kissed her cheek. "Okay, but I'm bringing you something back."

"Sure," she whispered. She sank tiredly into a chair next to J.C.'s bed and took the almost lifeless hand of her lover into her own. She would give her own life if it would only bring J.C. back. She swallowed the lump in her throat, refusing to dwell on the possibility of J.C.'s dying. They were stronger than this. J.C. had to draw on their love to see her through. Their future lay before them, beckoning them to the life together each had been denied for so long.

She pushed the hair back from J.C.'s brow. The cast-laden arm was suspended next to the feeding tube. She watched J.C.'s chest barely moving. If one weren't paying close attention, it could go unnoticed. A chill came over her. The icy silence of death permeated the room. Her own chest felt like it would explode under the weight of her distress. She squeezed her eyes shut for a few moments, then popped them back open, staring silently at the face she so loved. Fresh tears, tears from deep within her soul, began to freely flow from her eyes. "Please don't die," she sobbed.

Ted quietly walked back into the room and knelt beside her. She threw her arms around his neck, burying her face in his chest. Jo and Rachel tiptoed into the room. Jo set a cup of coffee and a sandwich on the table.

Samantha composed herself. "Jo, why don't you and Rachel get some rest?"

"What about you?" Jo asked in a concerned tone of voice. "If you don't get some sleep, you'll get sick. Then how are you going to take care of J.C. when she wakes up?"

Samantha put her arms around Rachel and Jo. "You two are the best friends anyone could ever have."

Jo smiled. "All I know is the way J.C. has always felt about you, Samantha. I knew you had to be pretty special, and I found out she was right." She turned to Rachel. "She also was the one who set me straight about what I was doing to you."

"We've got to plan a special homecoming for her as soon as she gets out of here."

Samantha started to open her mouth, but Rachel quickly silenced her with a quick shake of the head. "She's going to get better."

Samantha hugged her. "Thank you, Rachel."

"Are you sure you'll be all right? We can stay," Jo assured her.

Samantha emphatically shook her head. "No, you two have been wonderful. But please, get some rest. I promise that I'll sleep here."

"I'll be back first thing in the morning," Jo said.

Samantha turned her attention to Ted. "I want you to get some rest, too. I'll be okay. I promise." She pointed to the coffee and sandwich sitting on the table. "I'll eat, then have the nurse bring in a cot for me."

He reluctantly picked up his jacket and slung it over his shoulder. He eyed her suspiciously. "You'd better do as you promised."

"I will."

After they left Samantha listened to the nighttime hospital sounds, feeling like she was in another world. This couldn't really be happening to her.

She closed her eyes for what she thought were only a few seconds, but was actually three and a half hours. She stirred when she heard someone come into the room. She stretched her aching, cramped body.

"Dr. Goston!" She was immediately on her feet. "What's wrong?"

He frowned. "She's developed a fever and a slight case of pneumonia." His voice was grave.

"She'll be all right, though?"

"I'm going to be perfectly frank with you, Samantha," he said wearily. "Her prognosis is not good. I don't know if she has the strength to fight this infection."

Her eyes flitted back and forth. "I don't care what it costs, do anything you have to."

"Samantha," he said in a low voice. "We've been doing everything humanly possible. Money's not the issue. It's out of our hands. There's nothing more, medically, that can be done for her."

"No! Do something!" she moaned.

He held her against his large chest, as her legs grew unsteady with her uncontrollable trembling.

* * *

Samantha woke with a start. Her neck ached from the precarious way she had laid her head next to J.C.'s in the wee morning hours, the hours after Dr. Goston left her alone to face her pain. She rubbed the back of her neck, then kissed J.C.'s almost lifeless lips. She turned and stood up on unsteady legs.

Jo was immediately at her side. She looked at the stale sandwich and cold cup of coffee still sitting where she had left it the night before.

"I couldn't eat," Samantha whispered. "In the night . . ," her voice trailed off.

Jo nodded. "I know. Why didn't you call?"

"I couldn't, Jo. I needed to be alone with her. If she died . . ." She broke down into sobs before she could finish the sentence.

"I'm going to stay with you and J.C."

"No, Jo. You need to go to work. What about Rachel?"

"I'm staying," she said adamantly. "Rachel will be back after work, and I'm sure Ted will stop in today." She looked at the cards adorning the walls of the room. "She always thought no one cared. Wait till she sees all of these. Christy wanted to come for a visit, but I asked our AA friends to wait until J.C. gets stronger."

Samantha stared in wonder at her. "Jo, do you know what you're saying? She's taken a turn for the worse."

"I won't believe it! No one knows J.C. like I do. She's a survivor, a fighter. Believe what you want, Samantha, but J.C. will pull through." Her jaw was set defiantly.

Samantha ran her hand through her hair. "Where do you get the strength, Jo?"

"From J.C." She looked into her eyes. "And that's where you should be getting it from, too."

"I finally can understand J.C.'s and your love for one another," she whispered.

"Thank you, Samantha." Her voice grew serious. "You do know that the night you found us together we were two lonely, scared friends reaching out to one another, trying to recapture our innocence."

"I do understand, Jo. It's made all of us stronger."

"Tonight you're coming home with Rachel and me."

"Let's just wait and see what today brings first," she answered.

"Samantha, would you like to freshen up?"

"I'll step into the bathroom and splash some water on my face."

Jo walked over to the bed, bent down and stared into the seemingly lifeless face of her friend. "Don't go, J.C.," she whispered. "We need you." She caressed J.C.'s cheek with the back of her hand as she continued to stare. She placed a hand on J.C.'s brow. "Come on, open your eyes, dammit!" she muttered. She stared at the still—closed eyes, then saw a faint movement. She removed her hand. J.C.'s face was as it had been for the past three days. Silent. She looked closely again. There! She saw it again. An eye was trying to open! She was certain of it. She rubbed her own eyes to make sure that they weren't playing tricks on her. She kept her eyes glued on J.C.'s eyes. The eyelid was moving rapidly.

"Nurse!" Jo shouted into the intercom.

Samantha rushed out of the bathroom, her face ashen. "What's happened?"

Jo grabbed her shoulders excitedly. "Her eyes," she panted. "She's trying to open her eyes!"

Samantha's gasped. "Jo, she's going to make it!"

A nurse ran into the room, followed by Dr. Goston. "Her eyelids moved! Twice!" Jo cried.

"Let's take a look. It could just be a reflex. We can't get our hopes up."

"No, she's trying to open her eyes," Jo insisted.

"J.C.," the doctor called. "J.C., can you hear me?"

They waited in silence, then all four watched as an eyelid twitched, slowly began to open, and just as quickly closed again.

"J.C.," Dr. Goston called. "Can you open your eyes?"

Her hand trembled slightly. Samantha grabbed J.C.'s hand, bringing it to her own face, wetting it with her tears. "Look at me, J.C.," she pleaded.

Her eyelids fluttered, then opened and closed.

"J.C., do you know where you are? Can you hear me?" Dr. Goston called.

Her eyes slowly opened. For the next ten minutes they opened and closed, then finally stayed open for a few seconds before closing again.

"J.C., can you move your hand?"

All eyes turned to Samantha as the hand she held in her own weakly closed around Samantha's fingers.

The doctor lifted her eyelids and examined her carefully. "She may have vision problems for awhile, but everything looks clear."

"What are you saying, Dr. Goston?" Samantha asked hopefully.

He smiled broadly. "I have every confidence that she's going to recover. Her fever's gone and her lungs are clearing. She's tough."

Samantha looked back to J.C. "But she's not waking up," she insisted. "Why isn't she waking up?"

"It's going to take time. Maybe weeks," he assured her. "She's been through an ordeal, and the infection hasn't helped."

"Will she be as she was before?" Samantha asked in a low voice.

The doctor removed his glasses. "We need to take this one step at a time, Samantha. She may not open her eyes fully for some time, and she's going to be extremely weak."

Samantha continued to hold J.C.'s hand. "Could she have a relapse?"

"That's possible, but not probable." He studied her tired, worn face. "You need to get some rest or you'll end up in here . . . as a patient."

"I'm fine," she promised him.

He turned to Jo. "Talk some sense into her."

"I've tried."

"I'll check back in a few hours. Meanwhile I'll have a nurse stay in the room with her."

"Thank you, Doctor."

Jo placed a hand on her back. "Let's go to my place, Samantha." Her voice was compassionate. "Let me fix you some food," she prompted. "J.C. will never forgive me if you get sick," she added. "She would do the same for Rachel if the situation were reversed."

Samantha fought the turmoil within herself. "You'll bring me back later?"

"You bet I will." Jo gave her a friendly smile. "You'll feel better after a shower and some hot food. And a few hours of sleep wouldn't hurt."

"I'll be notified if there's any change?" She searched Dr. Goston's eyes.

"Samantha, how long have you known me?"

"All right then. I'll go for a few hours."

The doctor winked at Jo, then left the room.

CHAPTER TEN

Samantha spent the next few days in a mental fog. J.C.'s progress hadn't advanced beyond her fluttering eyelids or a slight, occasional movement of her hand. She spent her days with J.C. and only left her side when Jo and Rachel lovingly forced her to, Her fear of losing J.C. refused to shake its grasp on her. She worried if J.C. should awaken in the night and she wasn't there. She wanted to be the first person J.C. saw when she fully opened her eyes. J.C. looked so vulnerable and helpless lying in the bed. Samantha yearned to be held in her strong arms once again and to hear her words of love whispered to her in the still hours of the night.

The police were at a dead end in their investigation. No one had seen or heard anything unusual. The only positive report came from the receptionist, Karla, but no one knew who the visitor to J.C. was that day at the factory. After the visit, J.C. went back to work, not making mention of the stranger.

Samantha sat holding her hand. Jo and Rachel had gone to a meeting but would arrive in an hour or so to pick her up. Then tomorrow she would continue her vigil. Nothing mattered to her now, only J.C.'s returning to her. She rubbed J.C.'s hand with her thumb and looked into the quiet face. "If you hear me, J.C., please give me a sign."

She waited for five minutes and had only briefly closed her eyes when she felt movement in her hand. She opened her eyes and looked down. J.C.'s fingers were trying to grasp her hand. She jumped up, still holding J.C.'s hand in her own. "Honey," she whispered. "Can you hear me?" She searched her lover's face. J.C.'s eyes fluttered. But this time it was different. They didn't stop after a minute or two. Samantha's heart swelled with anticipation as she closely kept her own eyes focused on J.C.'s. She watched for ten full minutes. "Open your eyes, baby. Come on, you can do it," Samantha coaxed refusing to remove her eyes from J.C.'s. "You can do it. Open your eyes, honey."

J.C.'s lips parted, then her drooping eyelids sluggishly rose.

Samantha's heart leapt. "J.C., I'm here," she said softly. "Open your eyes for me."

J.C.'s lids rose.

Samantha stared into the silent eyes. "Oh, baby," she sobbed. She watched, waiting for the lids to drop back down, but this time they didn't. They stayed open. She grabbed the buzzer.

Seconds later a nurse rushed to her side. "Let me page her doctor."

She quickly returned with Dr. Goston at her heels. "Are her eyes still open?"

Samantha nodded.

Dr. Goston bent over her. "J.C., can you see anything? If you can, squeeze my hand." He placed her hand over his. Her fingers lightly pressed against his. "Are you in pain? Squeeze my hand if you are." They waited, but her fingers remained relaxed. "It's going to take time, J.C., but you'll get your strength back." He turned to Samantha. "I expect her progress to be rapid from here on in, but don't become alarmed if she stays in a lethargic pattern for awhile."

"How long do you think it'll be?" Samantha questioned.

He shook his head. "It could be days, weeks, or even months. Her body has been through a horrible shock."

"I understand."

Jo and Rachel walked into the room. Upon seeing the group surrounding J.C., Jo rushed to her side. "What's happened?" she asked in a shaky voice.

Samantha grabbed her. "Jo, look!" she excitedly pointed. "She's kept her eyes opened. She can comprehend what's happening."

Jo beamed. "I knew she'd make it."

Dr. Goston turned to them. "She has a strong will to survive."

Samantha spent the following weeks at J.C.'s bedside, coaxing her and guiding her.

J.C. could speak, but her words came slow. Samantha saw the frustration on her lover's face. "Don't worry, baby," she said. She spent tireless hours reading to her or just sitting, talking quietly. When J.C.'s IV's were removed, she patiently fed her. She saw the annoyance in J.C.'s eyes and it amused her. "Honey, how can you feed yourself with your arm in a cast?"

J.C. always answered with the half-cocked smile that went straight to Samantha's heart.

She thrived on her nightly visits from Jo, Rachel, Ted and the friends she had made in AA. Christy and Mark stopped in several times a week with assurances for her that her counseling job was waiting for her when she was fully recuperated.

The only questions J.C. bitterly refused to answer were the events leading up to the brutal attack on her. She adamantly squeezed her eyes shut and refused to talk. No prodding from anyone could get her to speak about that night. Dr. Goston assured them that this was normal. Her mind wanted to forget. She needed to heal first. They waited patiently until one day she looked at Jo.

"Do you remember my brother John?" she asked, pausing after each word.

The question caught Jo off guard. "Yes, I do, J.C." She searched J.C.'s face as Samantha looked quizzically at them. J.C. had never once mentioned her family by name to her. She had only referred to them as her brothers and sisters but gave them no personal identities. "J.C.," Jo said in a quiet voice. "Did Johnny do this to you?"

J.C. looked into her friend's caring eyes. "Yes," she murmured.

"That bastard!" She clenched her hands, as her jaw grew firm. "I'm calling the police. You've got to tell them everything, J.C.," she demanded.

"No."

"What the hell do you mean no?" she asked incredulously. "You can't let that scumbag get away with this!" Jo grabbed her hand. "Sweetie, he's not going to harm Samantha."

Samantha bent over her. "Talk to the police. Please? We need to have him arrested."

She nodded tiredly.

* * *

Jo and Samantha sat on one side of J.C.'s bed as Officer Donovan pulled up a chair on the other side. "Miss Markin—"

"J.C."

He smiled warmly. "All right. J.C., you told your friends that your brother Johnny Markin attacked you."

She nodded.

"Do you know what provoked his attack on you?"

"Money."

"Had you been giving him money in the past?"

"No, no. I hadn't seen him in almost ten years."

"Can you tell me everything that happened the day of your attack?"

She nodded again.

Jo and Samantha listened intently as J.C. relived her nightmare.

"I didn't want him to break Samantha's vases." Tears filled her eyes. "The last thing I remember is falling to the floor. He kept me pinned down and wouldn't stop punching me. I don't remember anything else. I'm sorry."

"You've given us everything we need. We'll find him," he assured her. He stood up, and then looked down at her. "I'll contact you the minute we have him in custody."

"Oh, baby," Samantha cried, cradling J.C. in her arms.

Jo angrily paced back and forth muttering to herself.

"Your vases," J.C. said softly.

"Forget about those damned vases, J.C. You're all that matters to me. Don't you know that by now?" She rested her head next to J.C.'s.

Two weeks later Dr. Goston found J.C. well enough to be released from the hospital. She grinned widely as Samantha, Jo, Rachel, and Ted became her entourage. Samantha unlocked the apartment door as Ted helped J.C. into the room.

"Welcome home!" a chorus of voices rang out in greeting.

J.C. looked at all of the faces coming towards her, giving her shoulder friendly pats. She smiled at Mark and Christy. All of her newfound friends were here. She tried to speak but found herself at a loss for words.

"That'll never happen again," Samantha teased as J.C. playfully tugged at her sleeve.

"Later I have an even bigger surprise for you," Samantha whispered in her ear.

"What?" J.C. asked.

"Now if I told you, it wouldn't be a surprise, would it?"

J.C. looked into Samantha's laughing eyes. "Not even a hint?"

"No, you'll just have to wait."

Ted led J.C. to the sofa, and Jo shoved pillows under J.C.'s cast-enclosed arm. She leaned back, enjoying the festivities in her honor. Her heart felt as though it would burst. She had never known so much happiness.

After the party ended and everyone departed, Samantha sat down next to J.C., draping her arm across J.C.'s shoulders and gazing into her eyes. J.C. smiled contentedly.

"I have something to say to you."

"What?" Her voice was low.

Samantha stroked J.C.'s shoulder. "I want a commitment."

J.C. grinned. "You're asking me for a commitment? You've had it from day one."

Samantha slightly tossed her head. "I want more," she said quietly.

J.C. raised her eyebrows. "Sam, it may have taken us a long time to get to this stage, but honey, no two people could ever be more committed to each other than we are."

"I want a committment ceremony, J.C. I want to marry you."

Tears brimmed in J.C.'s eyes. "I can't believe I'm hearing you say this. You don't know how long I've waited for this moment."

Samantha held her close. "Watching you day after day in the hospital, wondering if you could hear me, drove me crazy."

"I heard you," J.C. whispered.

"What?"

"I heard you, but I couldn't open my eyes to look at you, or open my mouth to tell you I loved you. I was trying to answer you. Even though my body was incapable, my mind was screaming out words. It was a silent cry to you."

Samantha brushed her lips against J.C.'s. "I have something for you." She took a small box from her pocket and quickly lifted the lid. Inside, nestled next to one another, lay two rings. "Marry me."

Tears overflowed from J.C.'s eyes. She was happy, truly happy. This love she had so desperately sought would always be hers. There would be no more standing on the outside looking in. She stroked Samantha's cheek. "We've been through so much the past few years. I thought I'd lost you forever, but now this is forever." She wiped the tears from her eyes. "I fell in love with you the first night I met you."

"I did with you, too, only I didn't know what it was at the time. All I know is that I don't ever want us to be apart again."

"Never," J.C. promised. "Never again."

THE END

5-DRON

Printed in the United States
1195200001B/189